Coop the Great

Yellow Dog
(an imprint of Great Plains Publications)
1173 Wolseley Avenue
Winnipeg, MB R3G 1H1
www.greatplains.mb.ca

Great Plains Publications gratefully acknowledges the financial support
provided for its publishing program by the Government of Canada
through the Canada Book Fund; the Canada Council for the Arts;
the Province of Manitoba through the Book Publishing Tax Credit
and the Book Publisher Marketing Assistance Program; and the
Manitoba Arts Council.

Design & Typography by Relish New Brand Experience
Printed in Canada by Friesens

LIBRARY AND ARCHIVES CANADA CATALOGUING IN PUBLICATION

Verstraete, Larry, author
      Coop the Great : a novel / Larry Verstraete.

Issued in print and electronic formats.
ISBN 978-1-77337-009-5 (softcover).--ISBN 978-1-77337-010-1 (EPUB).--
ISBN 978-1-77337-011-8 (Kindle)

      1. Title.

PS8643.E774C66 2018   jC813'.6   C2018-904160-9
                                           C2018-904161-7

ENVIRONMENTAL BENEFITS STATEMENT

Great Plains Publications saved the following
resources by printing the pages of this book on
chlorine free paper made with 100% post-consumer
waste.

TREES	WATER	ENERGY	SOLID WASTE	GREENHOUSE GASES
3	230	1	10	1,274
FULLY GROWN	GALLONS	MILLION BTUs	POUNDS	POUNDS

Environmental impact estimates were made using the Environmental Paper Network
Paper Calculator 4.0. For more information visit www.papercalculator.org.

Canada

FSC
www.fsc.org
MIX
Paper from
responsible sources
FSC® C016245

Coop the Great

the

Great

A Novel

Larry Verstraete

yellow dog

*For Benji, Bernie, Freckles, Roxy, Lilah, Hayley, Molly
and the other great dogs I have known and loved*

Prologue

Once, I watched a program on the Animal Planet channel. The Animal Planet wasn't one of the usual stops my owner-at-the-time made when he channel-surfed. He preferred sports, especially wrestling if that can be called a sport. But that day there wasn't much on TV. The program featured a dog. Near as I could figure, the dog was a mixed breed, probably cocker spaniel with a touch of German shepherd. I'm pretty good at telling one breed from another since I am a dog myself. Also, I have experience. I've lived so long and have been in so many homes and shelters that I've lost count.

But back to the TV program. Wires ran from the dog's head and chest to a panel of instruments. A woman in a white coat held photographs in front of the dog. In one photo, a man was smiling. In another, he was frowning. In a third, he appeared to be yelling. As each photograph was shown to the dog, a guy in another white coat watched numbers flash across a computer screen. A narrator explained that these people were scientists. They were conducting a study to find out if dogs favoured one face over another.

Humans have been wondering about dogs since the world started. If I had the ability to speak, I could have saved those scientists some time. We like smiling faces more than angry or upset ones, and most of us are a lot brighter than people realize. Granted, some dogs are dolts. Every species has its share, even humans. But most dogs are deep thinkers. We're better than people at a whole bunch of things like detecting odours, tracking sounds, and reading minds.

Actually, dogs don't really read minds, but we are very good at decoding clues. We follow hands. We watch faces. We listen carefully. We smell everything. We compile all the evidence in an instant. From there, we arrive at a conclusion. Come to think of it, we're not so different from those scientists with their fancy equipment.

In that TV program, scientists thought they were being clever. But I think they missed the point. They probably learned something about the dog's brain, but they learned nothing about what really mattered. Nothing about a dog's emotions. Nothing about a dog's character. Nothing about a dog's destiny.

Many people scoff at the idea that a dog can be anything more than a simple animal, but I know better. Even a runt like me can do great things.

I didn't always think this way. My outlook on life was sour for a long time, but I can pinpoint the moment I began to see things differently.

It all started at Derby on a Saturday that began like so many other Saturdays before.

Chapter 1

My last night at Derby Animal Shelter, I couldn't sleep. Not just because the room reeked of urine, thanks to Buck, my roommate. And not only because the fluorescent lights buzzed and flickered, casting creepy shadows across the cold concrete floor.

Of all the reasons I couldn't sleep, the thought of morning topped the list. Another open house. Another round of visitors sweeping through the building, eager to adopt a dog to suit their needs. Not too old. Not too short. Definitely not fat. Gotta be smart and oozing personality. The list was endless.

Derby Animal Shelter was a no-kill facility. More than a dozen dogs lived there. Some had strayed from their homes and were found wandering the streets. Others, like me, had been rejected by their owners. Across the hall, behind a cinder block wall, lived a gazillion cats. I'm exaggerating of course, but judging by the volume of the non-stop wailing coming from their quarters, it was an impossibly high number. Probably it was closer to thirty or forty. Too many.

Every Saturday, visitors paraded through Derby. Many peered into my room, shook their heads, and dropped comments as if I couldn't hear or understand. Worse yet, many laughed. "Look! A wiener dog! A sausage meister! A teenie weenie! Ha, ha!"

I knew what the visitors were saying. The way they sneered, snickered, pointed, rolled their eyes, and nudged each other with their elbows. I knew ridicule more than anything.

Ruth, the short lady with the braided hair and quick laugh who toured visitors through Derby, tried to cover for me. "His name is Cooper. He's a small dachshund. Dachshunds might look odd, but they make wonderful pets."

A wonderful pet. Me? You're kidding.

That night, Buck snored like a buzz saw. He was a recent arrival, not much more than a pup. Even though I tried to explain the routine to him, he just stared dozy-eyed at me. It didn't take long to figure out that although Buck had long legs and gorgeous brown hair with white markings, his head was hollow. Dumb as a cat, that one. And without much bladder control either.

When the first visitors arrived, Buck strutted past the window that separated our room from the hallway. I collapsed on my blanket in the corner, too tired to hope or care.

Within minutes, a couple with two kids stopped by. Buck wagged his tail, pranced and danced. Such a ham.

The boy tapped the window. The girl tugged the woman's sleeve. The lady shook her head, then shrugged. She nudged the man beside her. He leaned towards Ruth to say a few words.

When Ruth opened the door and led Buck into the hall, she glanced at me and shook her head. "Maybe next time, Cooper."

Not likely.

The little girl brushed Buck's silky hair. "He's so cute," she cooed.

"Please," the boy pleaded. "Can we keep him?"

"Promise you'll take care of him?" the woman asked.

They reminded me of my last owners. When they adopted me, they were happy and excited too. It didn't last long. A month.

I pushed back the awful memories. Some things are best left forgotten. Instead, I pretended to share Buck's joy. I wagged my tail and circled him.

"You're going to miss Buck, aren't you?" Ruth said.

Not really.

Of course, I couldn't tell her, at least not in words the way humans do. I couldn't tell that family what they were really getting. Dumb. Dumb. Really dumb.

By noon, the crowd had thinned. Only a few visitors trickled past my window. And then they stopped coming entirely. Silence settled along the hallway. I slept, exhausted from my long night of worry.

Then I heard the click of a latch. Down the hall, a door squealed open. Barks and howls erupted from every room.

Two figures shuffled into view. Ruth and a giant of an old man. He towered above Ruth, so tall he had to bend down to speak to her. They peered through my window. Ruth said something to the old man. He smiled, nodded, and rubbed a gnarled hand across his narrow face. A moment later, they moved on.

It was impossible to sleep now. Too much noise. Too much anxiety. I waited for the ordeal to end. Then, unexpectedly, I heard a tap on the window. Ruth and the old man had returned.

The man smiled and winked. Then he waved. He turned to Ruth to say a few words. Ruth frowned. She started to say something, then nodded.

Ruth opened the door and stooped to click a leash onto my collar. "Come, Cooper," she said, tugging me gently.

My legs ached, worse that day than some others. I shook off the stiffness, ignored the pain in my back, and wobbled after Ruth. Partway, I stopped. My blanket. I veered back and snatched it with my teeth. I followed Ruth into the hall, the blanket trailing between my legs.

Ruth smiled. "Almost forgot it, didn't you Cooper?" She shook her head. "He won't go anywhere without it."

The man reached down, then straightened again as if bending was too much of an effort. I examined his shoes, so large, so scuffed and weathered. I scanned higher, up his wrinkled pants, past his checkered shirt, way up to a head that seemed to touch the ceiling. A mop of grey hair topped a leathery face.

The man drew deep breaths as he squatted. It seemed to take him forever to fold his knees, and his joints creaked as if they needed a slug of oil to grease them.

With his face close to mine, I saw things I had missed earlier. Wrinkles creasing his brow. Skin sagging under his chin. Puffy tissue under his cloudy blue eyes.

You can tell a lot about a person by looking into their eyes. Human eyes are like windows without shades. They reveal a person's mood. With eyes, you can tell if the person is happy or sad, curious or bored, friendly or mean. The man's eyes shared their secrets with me. I found gentleness there, but also sadness.

"Hello Cooper."

The man caressed my ears with long, knobby fingers. He ran his huge hand along my back. Then he slid his fingers down my side, skimming the bald patch just above my rear leg.

The wound had healed months ago, but I flinched anyway. Call it instinct. Or maybe it was conditioning. Or was it habit? Humans have so many words to describe things.

"Cooper's been here a while," Ruth said. "Most people don't want an old dog, especially one with medical issues." She eyeballed me and lowered her voice. "He's a good dog, but he's had a rough go of it. The last adoption... Well, let's just say, there were a few problems."

The man nodded. He reached out and patted my head. "There, there," he said. His voice was soft but gravelly, as if his throat could use a drop of oil, too.

"Cooper keeps to himself. He's very quiet. I don't think he's barked once since he arrived here. I'm not even sure he can." Ruth looked at the old man. "I suppose that's a good thing."

The man smiled. I leaned into his hand. Then I stuffed my muzzle into his crotch and inhaled deeply.

Crotches are ripe places, rich in odours. Each

crotch smells special. They are as unique as finger-prints and the fastest way for dogs to know a person.

I'm not sure why, but many humans dislike this. They push away, leap back, or hold their hands in front of their crotch as if protecting something valuable.

Not this man. He let me linger. While I sniffed and memorized his features, he stroked my fur. His fingers skimmed my scar. This time I didn't flinch.

"There, there," he said again.

"Have you owned a dog before?" Ruth asked.

The man smiled. "No, can't say I have. I guess there's a first time for everything."

My heart stopped. A rookie. Wouldn't you know it.

Chapter 2

After filling out some paperwork, the old man and I were outside, breathing fresh air and sloshing through puddles from the latest downpour. The man had a strange walk. With each step of his right leg, he took two small ones with his left. He carried the blanket in one hand and gripped my leash in the other. We splashed along, my short legs barely keeping up.

Like teetering ships, we veered across the parking lot to the only car there—a rust bucket if ever there was one. The rear bumper was missing. A string of dents lined the trunk. A few dings pocked the passenger door. When the man opened it, a chunk of rust fell to the pavement.

He tossed the blanket inside. "Go ahead, Cooper."

I looked at the impossibly high seat. *You have to be kidding.*

The man chuckled. "Well, I guess you'll need a hand."

He reached down and scooped me up. As he hoisted me onto the seat, the colour drained from his face. He grabbed the door to brace himself. "Oh, my," he wheezed.

He stood there for a moment, propped up against the door, drawing deep breaths. Rain pelted his head, trickled down his neck, and soaked his jacket.

Slowly the colour returned. "There. That's better."

While he ambled over to the driver's side, I inspected the interior. Sun-bleached upholstery. Cracked vinyl dashboard. Chipped windshield. Shabby, just like the outside.

And filled with odours, too. Mostly the scent of pine from the tiny tree that dangled from the mirror. But there was also the delicious smell of bacon from a large paper bag on the back seat. And something else. A faint odour from the upholstery where I sat. I sniffed, inhaling the sweet aroma. Perfume. Very faint, but still there.

The man climbed in, dug his cellphone out of his pocket, and placed it on the console. Shifting gears, he screeched out of the parking stall and wheeled onto the street. The paper bag in the rear tipped. I glanced back just in time to see a head of lettuce and a brick of cheese tumble to the floor, followed by an entire chicken encased in plastic wrap. My mouth watered.

The windshield wipers fluttered briskly, barely keeping up with the downpour. The old man dodged puddles, weaved past slower cars, and steered around potholes. When he screeched to a stop at a red light, I dug my heels into the seat, but it was too little, too late. I slipped off, smacked into the dash, and slid to the floor.

"Sorry about that, Cooper." The old man leaned over to scoop me up. "I suppose I am a bit of a speed demon. I might have trouble walking, but put me behind the wheel and I am a NASCAR driver."

He returned me to the seat and ran his fingers over my ears. "Are you okay?"

I leaned into his soft touch. *Yeah. I'm fine. A little shook up, but I'll know better next time.*

"Guess we never had a proper introduction," the old man said. "I'm Michael." He looked at me, then shook his head. "Tell you what. We're both off to fresh starts. Forget Michael. It's Mike from now on. And you..." He rubbed his chin. "I think Coop is a better name for you. Mike and Coop. Yeah, that sounds right."

Sure. Why not? Add it to the list.

I've had many names. Oscar. Rusty. Flint. Clint. I forget the others. With each adoption, the new owner tried to erase the memory of the previous one. New name. New identity. Fresh start.

Coop? Yeah, I could live with that.

Mike rolled down my window and stuffed a cushion under me so I could hang my head out. "Go ahead, Coop. The air is free."

As we fired past rows of neat houses with carefully kept lawns, rain soaked my muzzle. Wind whipped my ears. A buffet of smells hit my nose—wet leaves, soggy grass, and, around one corner, the delightful scent of decaying compost.

We tore past a school, a grocery store, and several people huddled under umbrellas at a bus stop. As we rounded a corner, the phone rang. Mike glanced down and shook his head. He let it ring as he roared down the street. A few houses later, he slipped into a driveway and braked inches from a lopsided garage door.

"Jess? Is that you?"

A voice percolated through the phone. I cocked my head to one side to hear better but couldn't make out the words.

Mike frowned. He shifted the phone to his other ear. "Now, Jess. Slow down. Tell me again. Rick did what this time?"

The frown deepened. "What about Emma and Zach? Are they okay?"

They talked for a while longer. Mike said Rick's name several times, usually with a frown or heavy sigh.

"Do what you need to do, Jess." Mike said, ending the call. "Give my love to the kids."

He shook his head and stared out the window. Then he opened the door and shuffled around the car. "Go ahead, Coop." He lifted me up and plopped me onto wet grass twice my height.

I glanced back.

"Don't worry. I'll bring your blanket."

I thought of bolting. But really, where would I go? And why? At my age and with my legs, I wouldn't get far. Besides, Mike had my blanket.

As I trudged up the crooked steps to the front door, Mike watched, a smile on his face.

"Ready?"

Chapter 3

Mike padded across a worn carpet, groceries tucked under one arm. "What do you think, Coop? Look around. This is your house, too."

We passed a grandfather clock and a tall mirror in the hallway. I caught a glimpse of us. Giant Mike, his head scraping the light fixture. Me, a long tube of brown fur perched on stubby legs with a whip for a tail.

We wove through the living room on our way to the kitchen. Pictures hung at odd angles along the wall. A spiderweb clung to the ceiling. A clump of unknown material—hair or lint or thread—drifted across the floor. It snagged my underbelly before moving on.

In the living room, I passed a maze of furniture—sagging sofas and worn chairs, a cabinet littered with knick-knacks and pictures, a coffee table heaped with newspapers and magazines.

"Not much, is it?" Mike said from the kitchen. "There's work to be done here, that's for sure."

Mike spread the blanket on the kitchen floor. "This is as good a spot as any, Coop."

He dug into his pocket, rattling coins and keys. He pulled out a fistful of change and tossed it into a cookie jar. "Old habit," he said, smiling sadly. "When times were tough, we used the money for outings to the theatre."

We? Was there someone else?

Wrapped in my thoughts, I missed the clues. I didn't hear the pad of soft paws approaching. I didn't see the shadow looming over me. I didn't smell the distinctive odour that identified its owner.

A furry paw swiped my snout. An angry black mass pounced on my back. Instinctively, I backed away to protect myself.

Mike whirled around and laughed. He stooped to pick up my attacker. "I see you've met Lucinda."

Yellow eyes glared from a snarling face. *More bad luck. A cat.*

Mike cradled Lucinda in one arm. "Now, now. That's no way to treat our guest."

The cat squirmed, hissed, and twisted free. In a single move, Lucinda leaped to the floor while Mike grabbed the air behind her.

"Lucy! Don't you dare!" he yelled.

Lucinda landed, whisper quiet. Her belly hung an inch above the floor, supported by thick legs and paws the size of coasters. She was easily twice my height and length, maybe more, and probably double my weight.

Lucinda arched her back. Her coarse black hair stood up like prickly quills. Her tail waved above like a warning flag. She hissed, then strutted towards me, swiping with her claws.

I stepped back, but Lucinda kept coming. When she was a cat-length away, she stopped. She tilted her head to one side and stared. I could practically hear the gears in her tiny brain grinding. *Now, what is this? A large rat? No, a puny dog, I think.*

Lucinda stepped ahead, hissed, and swiped again. This time she clipped my ear.

"Lucy!" Mike yelled. He crouched to nab Lucinda but teetered and grabbed a chair to steady himself instead.

Lucinda looked at Mike. I scurried under the table. By the time Lucinda looked back, I was tucked into a tight corner under a chair.

Lucinda hissed and narrowed her eyes. She crept closer, so close I could smell the fish on her breath. Tuna, I think.

I squeezed my eyes shut, expecting another blow. I heard nails scraping, breath drawn in and out, a desperate meow, and then...*nothing.*

I looked. Lucinda stared back.

I don't think Lucinda knew her own size or how impossibly narrow the chair was that I was under. The front half of her body was jammed between two legs of the chair. The rear half stuck out. Lucinda was a prisoner, stuck half inside a cell, half out.

"Lucy, I expect better of you," Mike said, prying the cat loose. He pointed to a kennel on the far side of the kitchen. "You'd hate that, wouldn't you? Now behave yourself."

Lucinda nestled in Mike's arms and purred like an idling car. Mike didn't see the evil looks she shot at me.

"That's better." Mike waved to me. "Coop, come out. Lucy won't touch you now."

My ear stung, but it hurt less than the injury to my pride. Cornered by a cat. How embarrassing.

Chapter 4

For the rest of the day, I kept an eye on Lucinda. To my relief, she spent most of her time snoozing atop a tower in the kitchen that had been built out of tubes and covered with carpet.

As Mike moved about the house, I followed, dragging my blanket from room to room. With so much to smell, what was left of the afternoon passed quickly. The rain ended, clouds drifted away, and finally the sun emerged. It shone through the smudged kitchen window, warming the floor near Mike's feet as he stood at the counter peeling carrots. I basked in the sun on my blanket beside him. Lulled by the sound of chopping, I dozed.

Suddenly, the chopping stopped. I jerked awake. Mike was leaning against the counter, his face pasty white, the knife still in his hand. He closed his eyes, dropped the knife, then staggered to a chair. He clutched his chest and winced.

Slowly colour returned to Mike's cheeks. He smiled weakly, then picked up his cellphone and punched a few numbers.

"Hello," Mike said. "This is Michael Baron. I'd like to make an appointment."

Mike reached for the calendar hanging on the wall. "Yes. With Dr. Poon."

He shook his head. "No, it's not really an emergency, but the episodes are getting worse."

Whoever was on the other end asked lots of questions. "Just a few minutes ago," Mike said. "Three times today. Twice yesterday. Yes, some chest pain."

Mike ran his fingers through his hair. "Monday? That soon? Yes, I suppose that would work. Follow-up appointments? Sure. We may as well book them now."

He flipped through the calendar and circled dates. "Thank you. See you then," he said, ending the call.

For a long time, Mike stood at the counter, staring out the window. He sighed, picked up the knife, then put it down again. He swung around. "Come, Coop. Let me show you something outside."

I snatched my blanket, but Mike shook his head. "Maybe we should leave it here. We wouldn't want to get it dirty, would we?"

Dirty? Have you seen this thing?

The blanket had gone with me from one adoption to another. Every stain, every tattered corner, even the singed hole in the middle, told a story, my story. So did the odours the blanket held. The smell of my sisters and brothers. The fragrance of my cologne-drenched fourth owner. The reek of rifle oil and gunpowder from the hunter who was my sixth or seventh one, I can't remember which.

Mike smiled, folded the blanket, and placed it on a shelf beside the back door. "Trust me. It will be here when you come back."

I studied his eyes. I found trustworthiness there just like he said.

Mike opened the door to let me out. Behind the house, a brick path cut through clusters of flowers, trees, and sculptures made of stone and scrap metal. Mike wiped small puddles off a bench beside a pond in the middle of the yard. He sat down and watched as I wandered.

Dogs are like property owners. We pee to mark our boundaries and claim our territory. It's our way of saying to another dog, "Hey bud, I was here before you. This place is mine."

I sniffed around a statue of a fierce dragon spewing fire, then moved on to another statue that looked like a half-horse, half-man creature. Although I couldn't detect the presence of other dogs, I peed in four places far apart, generously soaking each to leave my mark. I left my final deposit near a statue of a bare-chested man with curly hair who was holding a lightning bolt in one hand.

Mine. Mine. All mine.

Only, I knew that wasn't completely true. Mike's place wasn't really mine. I was just a temporary visitor. Mike would tire of me soon, just like my other owners. But any place was better than Derby, even if it was only for a few days.

Once finished, I sat across the pond from Mike. "Come, Coop." He patted the empty bench beside him.

Instead, I lay in the grass. I rested my head between two flowerpots at the edge of the pond. A few weeks at most and then it would be all over between Mike and me. Hearts get broken when one gets too attached. Mine has, believe me.

A dragonfly hovered overhead, then zipped across the pond to settle on a sculpture in its centre. Resting on a small island of stone, a sphere the size of several beach balls rose above the water. It was a hollow globe, a shell of loosely woven metal strands. Inside, I counted four figures: a short woman; a tall man with his arm wrapped around her; and, standing in front of them, two young children, a boy and girl. The four figures wore bright smiles, as if the entire world was theirs, as if anything was possible. Just like my last owners.

Naturally, I hated them.

Chapter 5

After dinner and dishes, Mike watched TV in the living room. Lucinda stayed in the kitchen, snoozing atop her cat tower.

I dragged my blanket into the living room. Nestled between stacks of newspapers on the floor, I dozed as Mike flicked through channels. He finally settled on a show where contestants competed for prizes by swinging through hoops and leaping across a pool filled with sharks. After that, Mike watched a hockey game. When players messed up, he yelled at the TV set, waking me up often.

During the second period, the phone rang. Mike glanced at the clock. A frown creased his brow as he picked up the receiver.

"Jess, calm down," he said, leaning forward. "When did this happen?"

Mike shook his head as he listened. "Are the kids okay? Is Rick still there?"

A roar erupted from the TV. A player had scored a goal. The crowd stood up. An organ played. For a moment, the noise drowned out Mike's voice.

"Just a moment, Jess." Mike lowered the volume. Then he pressed a button on the phone and returned the receiver to its cradle. "Can you hear me? I switched to speaker phone."

I heard sniffles and a soft voice choked with tears. "I hear you, Dad."

Mike's frown deepened. "This is getting serious. Have you phoned the police?"

My head shot up. Police?

"I suppose I should," Jess said.

"Yes, you should. You have a restraining order, Jess. Rick should not be anywhere near you and especially not near the kids."

"I know, Dad," Jess sobbed.

I was torn. Half of me wanted to listen to Mike and Jess. The other half wanted to watch the game. My eyes drifted to the TV. I couldn't help myself.

Two burly players faced each other at centre ice. They held their sticks high. When the ref dropped the puck, one of them slashed the puck away. The crowd roared.

Mike grabbed the remote and muted the sound completely.

"Listen, Jess. Why don't you and the kids come for a visit tomorrow? I know it's a long drive, but it would give us a chance to talk. Maybe we can figure something out."

Jess sniffled. "I suppose we could," she said after a long pause.

They exchanged more words. I zoned out and focussed on two players who seemed to be arguing. One threw off his gloves. The other one raised his stick. I held my breath, waiting for a fight to erupt.

Just then, I heard my name mentioned. I cranked

my head around. Mike was standing now, pacing the floor, a smile on his face.

"You'll like Coop," Mike was saying.

He launched into a long description. "He's small, brown, with silky ears. Very quiet and well behaved." At one point, he chuckled. "He's not young anymore. But then, neither am I."

Mike ended the call shortly after. "Love you, Jess. Give Emma and Zach hugs for me."

"Love you too, Dad." Jess said. "I'll see you tomorrow."

I barely heard the last bit. My attention was on the ref who was trying to pry two squabbling players off each other.

Chapter 6

After the hockey game, Mike moved through the house, locking doors and turning off lights. He stopped at Lucinda's perch to pat her head.

"Goodnight, Lucy. Sweet dreams."

Lucinda meowed and rolled to one side. When Mike turned around, she hissed at me.

Mike climbed the stairs to the upper storey. The steps creaked under his weight and Mike's bones creaked in return. Partway up, he stopped to catch his breath before carrying on.

"Up here, Coop," he wheezed. "This is where you'll sleep."

Mike waited as I trudged up the steps towing my blanket. It trailed between my legs, making the steep climb even more difficult because I kept tripping over it.

"Sorry about that." Mike scooped up the blanket when I reached the top. "I forgot. It goes where you go, doesn't it?"

A long, carpeted hallway sliced across the upper storey. Bedrooms lined the sides, each one with its door open and its inside dark. Just past the bathroom, the hallway emptied into yet another bedroom. Mike's.

Mike flicked on a light and waved me in. "Look around. I'll be just a minute."

He disappeared into a small bathroom. I heard

him brush his teeth and gargle. "It is what it is," he muttered more than once.

Unlike the messy downstairs, the bedroom was spotless. A long, wooden dresser underneath a window occupied one wall. An immense bookcase lined a second wall while a large, plush bed filled a third. A table beside the bed held a clock, lamp, telephone, and two framed pictures.

I wandered to the bookcase to gaze at Mike's collection. I'd never seen so many books in one place. Most of my previous owners were computer junkies or TV addicts. They rarely read books, let alone owned them.

Mike emerged from the bathroom dressed in striped pyjamas. He stood in front of the bookcase, fingers tapping his chin. He scanned the titles. "Now, let's see what we have here. No, not that one. Or that." He glanced at me, then resumed the search, muttering to himself.

While Mike searched, I studied the pictures on the bedside table. A wooden frame held a photo of two figures—a young woman and a small girl, clutching hands. They looked a little like two of the figures in the globe outside. In another photo, an older woman with white hair and soft eyes smiled for the camera.

"Ah! Here's one." Mike pulled an enormous book off the shelf and carried it to the bed. He pulled back the covers and slid onto the mattress. The bed sagged under his weight. His feet hung over the end.

He tapped the mattress. "Up here, Coop.'
Really?

"You can do it, Coop," Mike patted the bed again and opened the thick book.

But I knew I couldn't. And I wouldn't. What was the point of such close contact?

I dragged my blanket to the middle of the room, spread it out with my teeth, and circled it before settling down.

Mike chuckled. "Suit yourself. It's getting late anyways. Maybe another time."

He put the book on the table and picked up the picture of the woman and young girl. He ran his finger across the glass, then put it down and picked up the picture of the woman with the white hair. He sighed. "It's been quite the day, Eva." He kissed the picture and returned it to the table.

Mike patted the mattress once more before shutting off the light. "The offer still stands if you change your mind."

In minutes, Mike's breathing eased. Then he started to snore. Not the buzz saw kind like Buck's, but softer.

Except for Mike's breathing and the chime of the clock downstairs, the house was quiet. Too quiet. I missed Buck, Max, Sparky, and the other dogs who had lived at Derby with me. Strangely enough, I missed Derby, too, with all its noise and confusion.

In the dark, in a strange place, it's easy to imagine things. Floorboards creaked down the hall. Lucinda? Was she coming for me? I breathed easier when I realized it was just a branch scraping the window.

When sleep finally came, I slipped into a dream.

Dogs everywhere. Sparky. Buck. Max. Me, too. And one cat. Lucinda. Like a queen, she ruled over us, snarling, hissing, and swiping to keep us corralled under chairs.

When that dream ended, another began. A party. A cake. A happy family. Then flames, scorching heat, and panic.

I woke up, my heart racing. It took a long while to fall asleep again.

Chapter 7

When Mike woke up, darkness still shrouded the room. He glanced at the clock and groaned softly. "Might as well get up."

Tossing aside blankets, he slipped out of bed. "Come, Coop. We have things to do."

Mike disappeared into the bathroom while I stretched on the blanket. Later, as we trudged down the stairs, Mike carried my blanket while I trailed behind, one slippery step at a time.

"Morning, Lucy," Mike said as he flicked on the kitchen lights. Lucinda yawned, then leaped to the floor. She crept between Mike's legs. When she spotted me, she scowled.

Mike spread the blanket on the floor. He eyed me, then Lucinda. "You both must be hungry."

He dished out food, some into Lucinda's shiny metal bowl beside her cat tower, mine into another shiny bowl on the other side of the kitchen. Lucinda charged to hers, sniffed it once, then wolfed down the whole works.

"Go ahead, Coop," Mike pointed to my bowl.

But I had needs more urgent than food. Didn't Mike know that?

I dashed to the back door and danced in a circle. "Oh, I see," Mike laughed. "I'm new to all this."

Outside, I bolted across the yard. I inspected the spots I'd marked the night before and refreshed them with new offerings. While I made my rounds, Mike sat on the bench and gazed at the globe. Finally finished, I rested in the grass by the pond, nestled between the same two flower pots as before.

A thin layer of dew covered the base of the globe. The sun glinted off the metal, deepening its rusty colour. Huddled inside the globe, the four figures looked even happier than the day before.

Mike didn't say anything. He sighed several times, got up to leave, then sat down again. Finally, he walked slowly to the garage. I tagged along.

"Sorry, Coop," Mike said as he opened the door. "It's not safe. You'll have to wait here. Or I can let you inside the house, if you like."

Inside? Alone with Lucinda? Not even if I was dying of hunger.

I curled up outside the garage. My stomach rumbled as saws buzzed and hammers pounded inside. When Mike finally emerged, his shirt was covered in grime. He brushed it off as he opened the door to let me in.

One whiff and my stomach turned. I almost puked. I tried to dash outside, but Mike had already closed the door.

Dogs are so much more considerate than cats when it comes to doing their business. Once we're properly trained, we take our private matters outdoors. We don't dump inside the house under the noses of our owners.

I held my breath as I passed the litter box. I felt Lucinda's eyes following me as I dashed to my bowl. Midway, I stopped. Even from a distance, I knew something was wrong.

My bowl was upside down. The food was gone.

When Mike entered the kitchen seconds later, he eyed the bowl. "My, Coop! You must have been hungry."

Lucinda leaped down, strode across the floor, and wormed through Mike's legs. When he stooped to pick her up, Lucinda glared at me. I swear I saw her smile.

Gotcha, she seemed to say.

Chapter 8

For the rest of the morning, my stomach made strange noises. Fortunately, I located a few bits of kibble Lucinda had missed. While I hunted for more, Mike roamed the house, straightening piles of magazines and dusting furniture. He even dragged out the vacuum cleaner.

Mid-morning, he flopped on the couch and put up his feet. "That did me in," he said. In moments, he was asleep. I dozed, too.

The sound of a car pulling into the driveway woke us up. Mike hauled himself off the couch and shuffled outside just as a tall lady with flowing blonde hair emerged from an SUV. She whipped off her sunglasses, tossed them onto the front seat, adjusted her sweater, and ran her hand down her black pants to smooth out the wrinkles.

Mike smiled. "Jess," he said, giving her a hug. "I'm so glad to see you."

A car door opened and a small girl spilled out. Her flip-flops snapped as she ran to Mike, and her dress swished against her thin legs. She wrapped her arms around Mike's knees and hugged him tight. "Grandpa, I missed you."

"Emma," Mike said, reaching down to pick her up. "I missed you, too."

He hoisted Emma up a few inches, groaned softly, then quickly put the girl down again. "My, you are growing like a weed. How old are you now? Ten? Twenty?"

Emma giggled. "Oh Grandpa, don't be silly. I'm only six." Her face brightened. "But I'll be seven soon."

I nudged Mike's leg, not wanting to interfere but feeling that I needed an introduction. Emma peered around Mike. "Is that Coop?" She squirmed to free herself from Mike's grip. "He's cute."

In seconds, Emma was at my side, mussing my fur and running her hands over my ears. She stopped when her fingers skimmed the bald patch. "What's this?"

"A scar. Nothing to worry about," Mike said.

Emma nodded. Then she was off, racing through the front door. "Lucy. Where are you?"

Mike smiled and turned back to Jess. "Emma's grown some, hasn't she?" The smile faded. "Are you okay?"

Jess's eyes welled. She brushed the side of her cheek. "I'm fine, Dad."

Mike frowned. He stepped closer and drew back Jess's hair. The frown deepened. "Rick did this?"

I peeked around Mike's legs to see for myself. A bruise the size of a fist covered Jess's cheek.

"It's nothing," she said, choking back tears.

"There, there." Mike hugged her again, longer this time.

Jess dabbed her eyes with a tissue and glanced at me. "So this is Coop."

Jess's eyes were like Mike's—kind and inviting. But there was sadness there, too. And hurt.

Jess knelt and patted my head while I stuffed my muzzle into her crotch and inhaled deeply. Like Mike, she didn't object. She let me linger. I liked her right away.

Mike peered past Jess. "How's Zach?"

Jess glanced back to the car. "A little more off than usual."

"Did Rick..?"

"No. Not this time."

As Mike walked with Jess to the car, he kept his arm around her.

"Zach, say hello to Grandpa," Jess said as she opened the door.

I wedged between Mike and Jess and peered into the car. A boy sat in the front seat. His head was tilted back. At first, I thought he was asleep, but then I noticed wires running from a cellphone into his ears. His head bobbed. The fingers on his right hand clutched a pencil while his left hand held an open notepad. I edged closer to scan the page and saw a drawing of a bearded man with a ponytail. His eyes were cold and narrow. His upper lip curled above teeth that were bared. I shuddered. It was a portrait of an angry person, not much different than one of my former owners, a guy who shouted often.

Jess tapped the boy on the shoulder. "Zach, come out, please."

A short boy wearing jeans and a black hoodie

emerged from the car. Mike held out his arms to give him a hug. "Zach, it's so good to see you."

Zach pulled the wires from his ears and pocketed the cellphone and notepad. His hoodie hung loosely over his head, partly hiding his features. I caught a glimpse of an unsmiling freckled face, a wave of dark hair, and eyes the same blue as Jess's. He hoisted a large backpack to his shoulders and brushed past Mike, ignoring his welcome.

Mike reached to grab the backpack. "Here, let me help you with those things."

But Zach waved him away. "I'm fine. I don't need your help." He looked across the front yard and grunted. "What a dump. Each time I come here, it looks worse."

I growled. Perhaps because Zach was being so rude. Perhaps because I felt Mike needed defending.

Zach swung around, saw me, and sneered. "That's your precious dog?" He laughed. "Well, that's got to be the ugliest one I've ever seen."

I lost it. I don't remember exactly what happened. One moment I was beside Mike, the next moment I was snapping at Zach's sneakers.

Zach laughed, louder this time. "Whoa! Coop's in attack mode. Oooo, I'm so scared."

Then, he kicked me. His foot struck my belly, grazing the scar. I tumbled over and landed beside Mike, whimpering.

Mike scooped me up. "Are you okay, Coop?"

I looked at him. *I am. Really, it only hurts a little.*

Jess stepped forward and grabbed Zach's arm. "What's gotten into you?"

Zach shrugged and pushed Jess away. "Don't touch me."

He stomped up the steps. "What a bunch of losers," he snarled as he disappeared into the house.

Chapter 9

Jess and the kids stayed for the afternoon. Mike made ham sandwiches for lunch, which Zach wouldn't touch. He sat at the table, cellphone in his hand, wires in his ears, sullenly swinging his legs and kicking the table. Jess didn't seem to notice his rude behaviour. More than once, Mike opened his mouth to say something, but never did.

After lunch, Zach moved to the living room and plopped on the couch. He heaved his feet onto the coffee table and channel-surfed. I steered clear of him and spent my time in the kitchen where Emma was smothering Lucinda with attention.

Emma dragged Lucinda everywhere. At one point, she wrapped a towel around the cat's head. "Lucy," she cooed. "Let's play. You'll be the baby. I'll be your mommy."

Lucinda squirmed and clawed the floor, but Emma held her firmly. When she called for me, I ducked under the chair, out of reach and out of sight.

Later, Jess and Mike carried steaming cups of coffee outside. I hobbled around the yard, stiff and sore from Zach's kick. While I inspected my morning offerings, Jess and Mike sat on the bench beside the pond and talked.

"Jess," I heard Mike say. "Rick is a loose cannon. You know what he's capable of doing."

"I know, Dad."

Jess drew a tissue out of her pocket and dabbed her eyes. "I've tried everything. I've changed the locks. I've installed a security system. I contacted the police after I talked to you yesterday, but that hasn't helped. I'm running out of ideas."

She turned to Mike. "Rick hasn't paid support for a long time. I have a decent job, but it's not easy making ends meet."

Mike nodded. "I can help with that."

Jess shook her head. "No, Dad. I appreciate the offer, but I need to stand up for myself." She touched the bruise on her cheek. "It's Zach I'm most worried about."

"He's taking it hard, isn't he?"

"Zach's a good kid. Really he is. It's just that he's been through a lot this past year. It's not just Rick either. He's fourteen. Look at him. He's small for his age."

Mike chuckled. "He'll catch up, Jess. I did. I was the smallest kid on the block until I turned sixteen."

Jess smiled weakly. "I guess, but it hasn't made things easy for him. Especially at school."

I knew what that was like—being a runt, taking abuse from others stronger and taller. For a moment, I felt sorry for Zach. But the ache in my side reminded me of his angry attack and all sympathy vanished.

Mike touched Jess's hand. "Have you considered moving? Perhaps if you were closer to me…"

Jess shook her head. "That's a big step. I can't just quit my job and run away from my problems."

"Maybe the kids should stay here then. I have lots of room and that way they'd be far from Rick. You'd have one less thing to worry about. It would give you time to check your options."

"I don't know, Dad. They'd have to switch schools..." Jess's voice trailed off. She patted Mike's hand. "Thanks for the offer, but I don't think it's necessary. I'll figure out something."

She shivered and checked her watch. "We should be going. It's a long drive and the kids have school tomorrow."

After Jess and the kids left, the house felt empty. Mike shuffled from room to room. He checked the calendar in the kitchen and sighed heavily. He wandered to the living room to watch TV, but that didn't last long.

"Come, Coop. Time for bed."

I limped after him. When we reached the stairs, Mike stooped to pick me up. "Let me help you, Coop."

One hand under my belly, one hand clutching my blanket, Mike carried me up the stairs. He moved slowly and twice he stopped to catch his breath. Five steps from the top, he teetered. He dropped the blanket, grabbed the railing, then put me down.

"Sorry, Coop," he wheezed. "I don't think I can do this."

After a moment of rest, he slowly mounted the remaining stairs. "Can you manage, Coop?"

Of course, I could. Not easily, mind you. My arthritis was worse than yesterday and the spot where Zach kicked me was tender. I moved slowly, my blanket clenched between my teeth and trailing between my legs.

While Mike changed, I spread the blanket on the floor. After he slipped into bed, springs groaning, mattress sagging, Mike patted the comforter. "Want to join me, Coop?"

Politely, I declined.

Mike shook his head. "Suit yourself. Whenever you are ready"

He picked up the thick book from the bedside table, then put it down again. "It's been a full day, hasn't it Coop? Maybe tomorrow."

That night, sleep eluded both of us. Finally, just after the clock chimed twelve times, Mike's breathing slowed, his thrashing ceased, and I knew he'd fallen asleep.

I envied him. Thoughts skipped through my head like ping-pong balls. I thought of Jess, Zach, and Emma and their difficult situation. I thought of Max, Sparky, and Ruth at Derby and wondered how they were doing. Mostly, though, I thought about Mike. Even from across the room, I could hear his ragged breath.

What was wrong with him?

Chapter 10

The next morning followed much the same pattern as the one before. First thing, Mike fed Lucinda and me. This time I gobbled down the kibble, not leaving a bite for Lucinda to claim. Then Mike let me out. He sat on the bench quietly gazing at the globe while I circled the yard and did my business. Later, he sawed and hammered in the garage while I snoozed outside the door.

In the afternoon, Mike donned a jacket and grabbed his car keys. He opened the back door, closed it again, and returned to the kitchen. He looked at Lucinda, perched on her tower. Then he looked at me, lying on my blanket in a patch of sunshine.

Mike shook his finger. "Lucy, I expect you to be nice to Coop. Coop, be nice to Lucy." Then he pointed to the kennel in the corner. "I'd rather not have to lock you away when I leave."

As soon as Mike closed the door, Lucinda leaped from her tower. She swaggered across the room straight towards me.

Lucinda was like one of those muscled wrestlers I'd seen on TV—the kind that wears a scowl, brags, and can't wait for the match to begin. That was Lucinda—big, angry, anxious to show how tough she was.

She hissed, snarled, and arched her back. She took another step and swiped. I dodged her claws and backed up to protect myself, but she kept coming. Finally, I scrambled under the corner chair, out of Lucinda's reach.

Lucinda planted her body in front of the chair to block my escape. And there she stayed for the rest of the afternoon while I cowered in the corner. If I even twitched, Lucinda forced me back again.

Time crept by. The grandfather clock in the hall chimed twice, then later three and four times. My muscles cramped. My mouth ached for water. My stomach rumbled. Where was Mike?

After an eternity, I heard a car pull into the driveway. Lucinda raced across the kitchen and leaped up her tower just as the kitchen door opened.

A chemical smell wafted through the kitchen. Mike shuffled across the room, a large plastic bag in one hand. He placed the bag on the counter and took out a box and several bottles filled with pills. "So. It's come to this," he said.

He leaned against the counter, not saying anything. It was as if he didn't remember that Lucinda and I were there. He didn't even notice I was at the water bowl, slurping like crazy.

Finally, Mike sighed. "It is what it is." He wandered to the living room, flopped onto the couch, and fell asleep with the TV on. I dragged my blanket over and flopped down, too.

The TV blared as time slipped away. Light faded. Darkness swallowed the room. My stomach screamed for food. My bladder begged for relief. In the kitchen, Lucinda meowed pitifully. She was probably hungry, too.

When the clock chimed eight, Mike woke up. He flicked on the light. He put his hand to his forehead and lay down again. "Better take it easy," he mumbled.

A little while later, he gripped the arm of the sofa, slowly found his footing, and took a wobbly step. "That's better."

It took Mike forever to reach the back door and even longer to feed Lucinda and me. As he climbed the stairs, he hung on to the railing and took one slow step at a time. Twice, he stopped to catch his breath.

"Eva," he said to the lady in the picture as he climbed into bed. "I'm not doing so well."

Mike kissed the picture, put it back on the table, then patted the mattress. "Give it a try, won't you, Coop?"

But I couldn't. And I wouldn't. I curled up on my blanket and rested my head on my paws, free from attachments I might regret later.

"Suit yourself." Mike said.

He shut off the light. It had been an exhausting day. First, Lucinda. Then the worry of Mike. But tired as I was, I couldn't sleep. Neither could Mike. He tossed around, fluffed up his pillow, muttered a few times, and finally turned on the light.

"You awake, Coop?"

He reached for the book on the night table. "Maybe we should read something." Mike held the book up for me to see. "The book is called *Everything Dogs*. Now let's see…"

He flipped through the pages. "Ah, here's something that might interest you. It's from a chapter called *Special Dogs*."

He lowered the book and glanced at me. "You're special, aren't you, Coop?"

People have called me 'special' before. Not that I have humans all figured out, but usually 'special' meant that I was less than normal. A misfit of some kind. But the way Mike said 'special,' I wondered if he meant something else.

"Let's begin." Mike adjusted his reading glasses, leaned into the light to see better, and started. "On September 11, 2001..."

He stopped and looked at me. "That was a terrible day, Coop. Truly tragic. But I have a feeling something wonderful will happen in this story."

Mike started again. "On September 11, 2001, Omar Eduardo Rivera was working on the seventy-first floor of the north tower at the World Trade Center in New York City. The blind man's dog, a yellow lab named Salty, was at his side..."

I looked up. A lab? Just like Sparky.

"That morning, hijacked planes hit the building. Smoke filled the seventy-first floor and chaos followed as people scrambled to flee."

The singed hole in the middle of the blanket suddenly looked larger, the edges more charred. I wasn't sure I wanted to hear the rest of the story.

Mike's voice rose and fell to the rhythm of the words. Soon, I was lost in the story. I pictured Omar and Salty. I followed their every move on that horrible day. I saw Omar as he released Salty, hoping that the dog might find his way down the stairs to safety on his own. I saw Salty when he refused to leave his owner. When Omar took Salty's leash again and let the dog lead him down the stairwell, I saw that too.

Down they went, one step at a time, with Salty calmly leading Omar through the smoke and past fleeing people. I held my breath when they became separated. I breathed again when Salty nudged Omar's leg to let him know he was still there.

Down, down, Salty led Omar. Down the stairs and out to safety on the street.

When Mike finished, he closed the book. "Pretty remarkable, don't you think, Coop?"

That night, dreams haunted my sleep. I dreamt of Salty. Only it wasn't Salty. It was Sparky from Derby who led Omar down the stairs.

When that dream ended, another began. The scene was familiar. A cake decorated with candles. A family singing. Then flames.

I woke up, trembling.

Chapter 11

During the week that followed, life fell into a series of routines. In the morning, Mike let me outside. Each time, I circled the yard the same way, stopped to deposit fresh offerings, and rested in my sunny spot near the pond to gaze at the hollow globe and its figures.

Most mornings, Mike sat on the bench for a few minutes before disappearing into the garage. I waited outside, curled into a ball beside the door. Sometimes, for a thrill, I chased birds that collected around the pond. For someone with hip problems, this was not a good idea. My joints ached for hours afterwards and not once was I quick enough to snatch so much as a feather.

Back in the house, Mike would sit at the kitchen table, the pill bottles, a glass of water, and the box before him. Each morning, he swallowed two pills and washed them down with slugs of water. Next, he would open the box and take out a small machine.

"Doctor's orders." Mike said the first time he used the contraption. "Twice a day, morning and evening, I'm supposed to take my blood pressure." He shook his head and sighed. "It's no fun getting old, is it Coop?"

Some mornings, Mike took me for a walk around the neighbourhood. We must have been a curious sight, giant Mike with his odd shuffle, tiny me with my short plodding legs. Together we cut through yards, circled blocks, crossed streets, and dodged screeching cars.

Although we never took the same route twice, I developed a mental map of the neighbourhood based on the sights, sounds, and smells we encountered. The roar of motorcycles told me we were nearing the garage beside the library; the smell of ginger and lemongrass that we were almost at the Asian restaurant. The flag fluttering in the breeze signalled that we were approaching the fire hall; the laughter of children that we were nearing a school.

Once we ran into a lady Mike knew. "Hello, Sophie," Mike said.

Sophie smiled, shifted the bag she carried to the other hand, and straightened the floppy hat that covered most of her grey hair. "Good morning, Michael. It's good to see you out and about."

Mike smiled. "Good to see you, too, Sophie. How are you doing?"

They talked about the weather, the potholes pocking the street, and the state of the world. Mike smiled often. So did Sophie.

All at once, Sophie adjusted her glasses and peered around Mike. The smile faded. She took a step back. "You have a dog?"

"Yes. This is Coop. He's a rescue dog."

Sophie's eyebrows shot up. "Rescue dog? I see."

While they chatted, Sophie kept her eyes on me. "I suppose a dog would be good company, especially since...."

She let the unfinished sentence hang in the air. Mike nodded. "He is."

"Well, that's good then. But he's a rather strange-looking dog. Somehow, I pictured you with a German shepherd or a border collie. You know, a dog with looks and substance, not a … not a dog like *this*." Sophie's eyes narrowed. She pursed her lips and cleared her throat. "He looks pretty old, too. Why…?"

Another unfinished sentence. But I knew what she meant. Why this dog? There must have been better choices. Younger dogs. More handsome dogs. Why this one?

Sophie put the bag down and reached to pat me, but Mike stepped in front and tugged on my leash. "We must move on, Sophie. So nice to see you."

Mike walked briskly, leaving Sophie standing, mouth open, at the corner.

"Never you mind her," Mike said when we out of earshot. "She means well, but …"

But what? Mike never said.

We walked home slowly. My mind replayed the conversation with Sophie. Why exactly did Mike pick me? What did he see that no one else did?

Chapter 12

While mornings were mostly awesome, after-noons were mostly awful. Often, Mike left the house. He'd be gone for hours, doing what I couldn't say. When Mike came home, he sometimes staggered into the kitchen, pale and weak. On those days, he smelled of chemicals. They reminded me of the soaps and disinfectants that my third owner used. She was a clean freak who scrubbed the floors every day. Often, she scrubbed me too.

On other days, Mike's clothes smelled of different things: bread baking, coffee brewing, and, quite often, the scent of grass and freshly cut flowers.

Before leaving, Mike would stand at the door, looking at Lucinda and me. He always delivered the same lecture.

"Lucy, I expect you to be nice to Coop. Coop, be nice to Lucy."

Without fail, Lucinda meowed and waved her tail, pretending she understood. But as soon as the door clicked shut, she would leap from her tower, swagger across the kitchen, and swipe me into the corner. She'd plop her huge body in front of the chair, blocking my getaway.

Mike never caught on to Lucinda's bullying. The moment the car slipped into the driveway, Lucinda raced to her cat tower. By the time Mike entered, she was on the top platform, pretending to snooze as if nothing had happened.

As much as I hated afternoons, I loved evenings. Right after scaling the stairs, after Mike changed into pyjamas, brushed his teeth, and gargled, I settled down for the night on my blanket while Mike phoned Jess. "How are you doing? And the kids? Are they okay?"

They would talk for a few minutes. Although I could not hear most of their conversations, Rick's name came up often.

Once, Mike asked to speak to Emma. His face lit up when she came on the line. But when Mike asked for Zach, he lost his smile. He shrugged his shoulders and shook his head. "Don't worry, Jess. He'll come around. It just takes time."

Each call ended the same way. "Good night, Jess. I love you. Give Zach and Emma hugs for me, will you?"

Right after, Mike would open *Everything Dogs* and pat the bed. "Come on up, Coop."

Of course, I politely refused.

"Suit yourself. The offer is open whenever you are ready."

Now, for my favourite part. Each night, Mike read to me from *Special Dogs*. I learned about Balto, an amazing Siberian husky, who led a team of sled dogs through a raging blizzard to deliver medicine to the desperate people of Nome, Alaska. I learned about Hachiko, a famous Japanese dog who walked to the train station every day for ten years after his owner died to wait for him to come home from work even though he never did. To honour Hachiko's loyalty, local residents put a bronze statue of the dog at the train station. Every April, they hold a ceremony to remember his faithfulness.

Mike read about other special dogs, too. All of them were brave and remarkable, and nothing at all like me.

Chapter 13

One morning after a restless night, Mike rose much earlier than normal. Darkness covered the room. Other than the grandfather clock sounding downstairs, the house was quiet.

Midway through brushing his teeth, Mike peered around the corner. "Coop, time to get up. I have something to show you."

In the kitchen, Mike downed his pills and took his blood pressure. He brewed coffee and poured it into a thermos. Then he grabbed a few doggie treats and tossed them into a paper bag.

Mike let me outside. While I circled the yard, he watched from the bench. For a few minutes, we sat in our usual spots by the globe. Under the glow of a full moon, light danced across the figures.

A breeze rustled the trees, tearing leaves off the branches. Mike zipped up his jacket and hugged his chest. "It's cool right now, but I hear we're in for a scorcher today, Coop."

He looked at the sky. "No clouds. Perfect. We should go. The sun will be rising soon."

He let me into the house and grabbed a few blankets. He added mine to the pile and scooped up the thermos and bag of treats.

"Lucy, I'm going out," he said to Lucinda. "Coop's coming. Do you want to come, too?"

Lucinda opened one eye, then closed it again. She didn't move a muscle.

Mike chuckled. "That's what I thought. Okay, but don't say I didn't invite you."

Soon, we were wheeling down empty streets, passing houses steeped in darkness. The moon seemed to be directing us, lighting our way as we wove through the quiet city. When we turned down the highway, Mike stomped on the gas pedal. I dug my claws into the seat and hung on.

We passed farm houses and rickety barns. Finally, Mike slowed and turned a corner. We drove down a narrow gravel road, climbed a steep hill, and entered a clearing.

"We're here." Mike turned off the engine and shut off the lights. "Come."

He grabbed the paper bag and thermos and scooped up the blankets in the back seat. He walked to the edge of the clearing, spread out two blankets—his and mine—and sat down, his knees creaking.

"Join me, Coop," Mike said, patting my blanket.

A cold breeze sent shivers through my body. Why not? Just this once.

I snuggled beside Mike, grateful for his warmth. Mike tossed a blanket around the two of us and rubbed his hands together.

A sliver of pink appeared along the horizon. "We're a little early," Mike said. "That's okay. There's lots to see."

He pointed up. "Look there, Coop."

Thousands of stars dotted the sky. I followed his

gaze to a cluster above the horizon. "There. That's the constellation Orion, the hunter."

To me, the stars looked like tiny lightbulbs scattered across the sky. I couldn't tell one cluster from another.

Mike laughed. "I couldn't see Orion the first time either. But look again. See those seven stars. Notice how four of them mark the corners of a rectangle. Now look inside the rectangle. Do you see three stars that form a straight line? That's Orion's belt."

This time, I concentrated. Sure enough, there it was. Orion's belt.

Mike smiled and ran his fingers over my ears. "Pretty amazing, right?"

Mike pointed out other stars and constellations. Slowly, the sliver of pink along the horizon grew into an orange band. As the sun rose, I could see that we were perched on the edge of a ridge. Below us, a field of wheat waved in the wind.

"Ah, there it is. This is what I wanted you to see." Mike pointed to the spot above the horizon where orange met the blue-black sky. "Do you see it?"

I didn't. Not at first, anyways.

"See that star. The brightest one in the morning sky?"

I studied the spot. One star flickered brighter than the others.

"That's Sirius, the Dog Star."

Dog Star?

"If you look closely and use your imagination, you

can see that the stars around Sirius form the shape of a dog. That's the constellation Canis Major, the Big Dog."

I guess I didn't have Mike's imagination. A dog in the sky? Really?

Mike held me closer. "To ancient people, Sirius was special."

As the sun climbed higher, Mike told me a story. "In India, Sirius had another name. He was known as Svana, the dog of Prince Yudhistira."

Mike stroked my ears as he told the story of the prince and his faithful dog. I relaxed with my head in his lap and closed my eyes. In my mind, I saw Prince Yudhistira and his dog Svana. I saw them together on their quest to find the kingdom of heaven.

"In their search for heaven," Mike said, "Svana and the prince were joined by the prince's four brothers. They travelled far and wide. One by one, his brothers grew weary and gave up. Before long, only the prince and Svana were left."

Mike shivered and drew me closer. "Prince Yudhistira and Svana continued the search on their own. Eventually, they reached the gates of heaven. Their hearts were crushed when the gatekeeper refused to let Svana in."

I looked at Mike. *What? Dogs aren't allowed in heaven?*

Mike smiled. "The prince was dismayed. His brothers had deserted him, but Svana had stayed by his side throughout the long journey. The prince told the gatekeeper that if his good and faithful friend Svana wasn't allowed into heaven, then he didn't want to be there either."

Mike paused. I squirmed. *Go on. Then what?*

"This is what the gatekeeper wanted to hear. He told them, 'You are both welcome in heaven.' Then he opened the gates and ushered them inside."

Mike pointed to the constellation. "And there is Svana now. Only we call him Sirius here. Either way, he's shining bright for all to see."

I looked again, squinting as I studied the stars. This time, I saw it. Canis Major, the Big Dog. How did I miss it before?

Mike opened the thermos and poured coffee into a cup. He took the doggie treats from the bag.

"This place is special to me," he said quietly. "This where I proposed to Eva. Today would have been our forty-seventh anniversary."

He gave me the treats and held the cup up high. "To you, my darling. We had a good life."

We sat in silence, watching the sun rise and the stars fade. I thought about Eva. Like Sirius, she had been a good and faithful friend. Was she in heaven? Was she one of the stars now?

Chapter 14

A few days later, Mike woke up early again. He slid out of bed and dressed quickly. Downstairs, he made coffee and let me out. While I circled the yard, he sat on the bench.

The sun was just rising and each blade of grass shimmered with dew. As the sun rose, the four figures inside the globe reflected different colours—first pink, then orange, then red. They looked somehow happier and closer than ever before.

Mike pointed to the other statues scattered around the yard. "Eva loved this place. Near the end, she came here often to do just what we're doing, Coop."

Mike reached down to pluck a weed and straighten a row of stones. "We can't change the past, Coop. We can only move forward." Then he stood up and went into the garage.

Later, after much clanging and banging, Mike emerged carrying an object wrapped in a tattered blanket. "Come, Coop. I have something to show you."

He weaved across the yard, past the dragon figure, past the half-horse man to my sunny spot near the pond. "Ready?"

He tore off the blanket and placed the object on the ground. I stared blankly at a metal sculpture of a small dog. A star floated above the figure, attached with thin wire to the dog's head.

Mike raised an eyebrow. He placed his hands on his hips. "Well, what do you think?"

I looked at the figure, then at Mike. What was I supposed to make of this?

"It's Sirius," Mike said.

The sun glinted off the polished metal, adding even more brightness to the figure. I sat down, uncertain how I should react.

The dog looked just like me. Long body, floppy ears, thin tail. And along its hindquarters, a patch forged out of a different colour of metal. My scar.

It was me. It couldn't be anyone else.

I looked at Mike, confused by his gesture. *Why?*

Mike smiled. He reached to pat my head, "Stay as long as you want," he said. Without another word, he returned to the house.

I lingered. Sophie's shrill voice came back to me. "Somehow I pictured you with a German shepherd or a border collie. You know, a dog with looks and substance, not a … not a dog like this."

Did Mike think I was like Sirius? Did he think I could earn a star of my own?

Poor Mike. He couldn't be more mistaken.

Chapter 15

That afternoon, Mike left in a rush, abandoning stacks of unwashed dishes on the counter. As soon as the door clicked shut, Lucinda hurried over, ready for battle. I scooted into the corner. Like always, she plunked her body in front to box me in.

The grandfather clock ticked away an hour, then another. My muscles stiffened. My mouth felt like sandpaper. While I pretended to sleep, Lucinda roamed the kitchen. I opened one eye to watch.

Lucinda lapped water from her bowl and glanced back at me. Then, in one leap she bounded up onto the kitchen counter. I'd never seen Lucinda do that before. Had Mike been home, I am sure he would have shooed her away.

Lucinda padded across the counter. She poked her head into dishes and bowls. She lapped up leftover pancake batter and nibbled on a piece of bacon.

While Lucinda was busy, I crept out of my corner. I edged across the kitchen, aiming for the water bowl. With her head jammed in a large open jar of Cheez Whiz, Lucinda didn't notice me.

Partway there, I stopped. I thought of the dog statue outside. What would Sirius do in this situation? Head for the water bowl to satisfy his thirst? Or something else?

Mike wasn't here to enforce the rules. But I was.

Lucinda didn't hear the clip of my nails on the floor. Over the aroma of processed cheese, she didn't smell my scent either. Her tail hung over the counter, swinging like the grandfather clock down the hall. Swish. Lick. Swish. Lick. She didn't know I was there, watching from below.

I barked. Then I barked some more.

I couldn't remember the last time I'd barked. Frankly, my voice sounded deeper and stronger than I remembered. More like a big dog than a weenie one.

Lucinda jerked her head out of the jar and hissed. Bits of gooey cheese whipped around the kitchen. The jar spun like an out-of-control top. It hit the bowl of batter, spilling it on the counter. Batter pooled around Lucinda's paws and under her sagging belly.

I scrambled to the far side of the kitchen, back to safety under the chair. From there, I watched the scene unfold. It was a little like watching a movie in slow motion. Lucinda crouched to pounce. She slipped. She slid through the batter. Her heavy front end hovered for a moment over the edge of the counter, and then....

In the end, gravity took over. Lucinda careened off the counter at the same time as a large bag of flour tipped over. When Lucinda landed, flour rained down upon her. The flour made the floor slick. Lucinda backpedalled to regain control but couldn't. She shot across the kitchen like one of those hockey pucks on TV. Only there was no ref blasting a whistle and no goalie in the net to stop her.

There was, however, a shiny metal bowl filled with water.

When Lucinda slammed into her bowl, water sprayed across the kitchen. Combined with the flour, it made a sticky paste. The goo dripped from Lucinda's ears. From her nose. From her tail. It was all over.

Lucinda lifted one sticky paw, then another. For a time, she sat in the mess, too stunned to move. She looked to me, then to the counter, then to the floor as if she was replaying what happened. Finally, she pounced up to the top of her tower.

For the rest of the afternoon, Lucinda licked and licked, first her paws, then her tail, then her thick underbelly. Hours later, she still looked like a ghost.

I felt strangely satisfied by the experience. Even brave. I crept to the centre of the kitchen and found a spot untouched by batter or flour. In full view of Lucinda, I lounged on my blanket. She eyed me, hissed once, then returned to her licking.

For hours after, I replayed the scene. I didn't notice the patch of sunshine vanishing. The clock chimed seven times. Where was Mike?

By the time the car pulled into the driveway, milky darkness covered the room. I wandered to the door and waited. But Mike didn't come. Not for the longest time.

When he finally opened the kitchen door and flicked on the light, I was shocked by his appearance. His shoulders sagged. His hands hung limply at his side. His eyes looked dull and lifeless. The smell of chemicals seeped across the room.

Mike stared at the mess. "What the…" he sputtered. He held on to a chair as he surveyed the damage. He looked at me—flour-free. Then he looked at Lucinda—ghostly-white.

"Lucy," Mike said, wagging his finger. "What have you done?"

He shook his head. "I can't deal with this now."

Mike shuffled to the cupboards, opened a door, and pulled out a mug. He filled the kettle with water, then stood at the window and stared outside into the fading light.

Sounds leaked into the room from outside—the whoosh of traffic along the street, the groan of trees waving in the wind. The grandfather clock sounded louder than usual. When it chimed on the hour, I counted. Eight…nine…

Mike muttered something, but I only heard bits. *Worse… Not enough time…*

It took Mike an hour to clean the kitchen. It took him another hour to clean Lucinda. While he scrubbed Lucinda in the bathtub, she struggled and meowed pitifully, but Mike rubbed and brushed until every glob was gone.

That night, Mike fell asleep as soon as he hit the pillow. There were no goodnights, no stories from *Everything Dogs*. His breathing grew laboured. He twitched and turned. He called out Eva's name. Another time, he sat straight up, eyes open wide but seeing nothing.

Midway through the night, I did something I swore

never to do. It was not easy and I failed more than once. But with each failure, I learned something new.

On my fifth try, I raced across the room to gain momentum. Once near the bed, I leaped. I dug my claws into the folds of the comforter. I hauled myself up with my blanket clenched in my teeth.

I curled beside Mike and rested my head on his chest. He flung his arm around me. Gradually, his breathing slowed. His stirring ceased.

It took forever for me to fall asleep, though. Even after I finally did, I woke up often to dreams of ghosts that looked an awful lot like Lucinda.

Chapter 16

Mike slept in. Light was already streaming through the curtains when he tossed aside the comforter. He yawned and stretched, then he spotted me.

"Well, what do we have here?" He smiled and patted me. "Good morning, Coop. Glad to see you made it."

When he left that afternoon, Mike locked Lucinda in the kennel, but he allowed me to run free. I tried not to gloat, but it was difficult. I had emerged from the disaster victorious. Lucinda had lost the battle for once.

For days after, Mike locked Lucinda in the kennel whenever he left the house. At the end of the week, Mike delivered a final lecture. "Lucy. Have you learned your lesson?"

Lucinda meowed sweetly and curled between his legs.

"Well, I hope so. Let's try this once more then. No mischief or I'll have to lock you away again."

From then on, Lucinda spent most afternoons on her cat tower while I lounged on my blanket. When our paths crossed, she no longer hissed. Nor did she swipe. While she wasn't exactly being nice to me, she didn't torment me either.

Every night from then on, I slept beside Mike. Close together on the bed, we both slept better.

One night, Mike adjusted his glasses, leaned into the light, and opened *Everything Dogs* to a new page. "I think you'll like this one," he said.

He cleared his throat. "Once upon a time, long ago, a family in Silverton, Oregon had a dog named Bobbie."

Mike started almost every story with "once upon a time." Immediately, I relaxed. In seconds, Mike and I were both somewhere else.

Bobbie, I learned, was a two-year-old Scotch collie-English shepherd mix. Right then, I pictured Buck. He was a collie. Maybe Bobbie looked like him.

"Bobbie loved his family," Mike read. "He especially loved Tim, his owner. Wherever Tim went, so did Bobbie. Then one summer, Tim drove the family to Indiana for a vacation. Of course, Bobbie went along."

Mike's gravelly voice softened a little. He dropped his hand and patted my head. "Somehow Bobbie became lost. Tim and his family searched everywhere for him, but he was nowhere to be found. The broken-hearted family was forced to return to Oregon without him."

As Mike read, I pictured Buck. Buck with his long legs and beautiful coat. Dumb Buck, lost and alone.

I glanced at Mike. *What happened next? Go on.*

As it turned out, Bobbie was a whole lot smarter than Buck. He missed Tim and his family so much that he walked through the desert, over the Rocky Mountains, all the way to Oregon, 2,500 miles away. It took him six months. Six months of trotting across eight states, through winter snowdrifts and down the streets of Silverton to Tim's doorstep.

Mike turned the page. "By then, the family had lost hope of ever seeing their beloved dog again. When Bobbie showed up, he was barely recognizable. He was scrawny. He was filthy. The pads on his paws had worn thin."

In my mind, I saw Buck, tired, dirty, skinnier than a milk bone. Buck plodding the last mile. Buck zeroing in on home like one of those pigeons I'd seen on the Animal Planet.

Mike shifted the book to catch the light and continued. "Bobbie became famous. People sent letters to Tim praising Bobbie. They called him a Wonder Dog. Bobbie was showered with medals, keys to cities, even a jewel-encrusted harness. Books were written about Bobbie's incredible journey. Films were made, too. Today, a statue of Bobbie stands outside his original doghouse in downtown Silverton, Oregon."

Another statue? I had a statue, too, though I couldn't see why. It's not as if I had earned it like Bobbie or Hachiko.

Mike ran his hand down my back, skimming my scar. "Pretty amazing story, isn't it, Coop?" Mike yawned and shut off the light. "Good night, Coop."

I was almost asleep when the phone rang. Mike bolted upright, switched on the light, and tore the phone off the cradle.

"Hello."

His eyebrows shot up. "Jess, slow down. What happened?"

Mike tossed aside the blankets and stood up. He

wobbled a bit, then sat down again. "I see. No, you did the right thing."

He glanced at Eva's picture. "Yes. For sure. Tomorrow. The sooner, the better."

After he hung up, Mike stared across the room. Finally, he shuffled to the bathroom. "Company's coming, Coop!" he said.

Chapter 17

J ess arrived late the next morning. Mike went outside to meet her. They hugged. "Sorry, Dad," Jess said, brushing away a tear. "This is a lot to ask of you."

Mike hugged her tighter. "Nonsense. I'm happy to help. Besides, now I get to spend time with my grandkids."

Emma barrelled out of the car, dragging a small pink suitcase speckled with glitter. She hugged Mike, patted me, then ran up the steps.

Jess rushed after her, catching Emma just as she opened the door. "Em, wait a minute. I can't stay. Be good. I'll call you every night."

The two hugged.

"Lucy, I'm here," Emma screamed as she raced into the house.

Mike glanced at the car. "Zach. How's he doing?"

"He's angry, of course," Jess said. "Even though he won't admit it, I know he's scared, too. Emma doesn't really know what's going on. She slept through the whole thing. She thinks staying here is a great adventure. But Zach..."

The car door opened and Zach stepped out. His hoodie covered most of his head, but not enough to hide the scowl on his face.

Zach slung a bulging backpack across his shoulder.

As he skulked by, I hid behind Mike and peered through his legs.

When Jess tried to hug him, Zach shrugged her off. "Leave me alone." He kicked a stone and sent it sailing across the yard.

"I'll call later," Jess said.

"Whatever."

Jess stared vacantly at the door long after Zach disappeared. Finally, she turned around. "I'm sorry, Dad."

"It's going to be okay." Mike hugged her again. "We're all going to be okay. You'll see."

"I know."

Jess pulled a large suitcase out of the trunk. "I really didn't know what to pack. They have enough for a few weeks anyway."

"Did you want to stay for lunch?" Mike asked.

"No. I think I should go. I have a long drive ahead and an early start at work in the morning."

She turned to walk away, then swung back to hug Mike. "Thanks again, Dad."

They stood that way, Jess in Mike's arms, for quite a while. "I better go," Jess said again.

She climbed behind the wheel, then stuck her head out the window. "I almost forgot. You'll need this."

Jess passed a large envelope to Mike. "I've called the school to let them know the kids are coming, but you'll need these documents when they register."

After Jess pulled out of the driveway, Mike watched the car fade down the street. Long after it disappeared, he staggered to the house, wheezing with each step. He leaned against the door frame, drawing deep breaths, and reached into his pocket for a small bottle. He fumbled with the lid, stopped when he couldn't open it, then tried again. Finally successful, he popped a small pill into his mouth.

Slowly, Mike's breathing grew normal. He smiled weakly. "That was a whopper, Coop."

When Mike stepped into the house, he wore a broad smile. He stood tall. He walked briskly. "Zach! Emma!" he shouted. "It's a beautiful Sunday. Let's go to the park."

Mike looked healthy and happy. But Mike was getting worse. He knew it, and so did I.

Chapter 18

We never did go to the park. Emma was game, but not Zach. He spent the day in his bedroom at the top of the stairs.

"Just leave me alone," he shouted when Mike called.

Emma shadowed Mike. While he prepared dinner, she set up a station on the kitchen floor. She dragged Lucinda to my sunny patch.

"Let's play, Lucy."

Lucinda squirmed and wailed, but Emma tightened her grip. She reached out to me. "You want to play too, Coop?"

Before I could scramble away, Emma grabbed my collar. She threw a towel over my back and tucked it under my belly. She wrapped another towel around Lucinda's head and propped the cat beside me.

"Lucy, you'll be the mommy. Coop, you'll be her baby."

Lucinda clawed the floor and whined. She tried to make a run for it, but Emma hauled her back.

"Come on, Lucy. Look at Coop. He's cooperating. Why can't you?"

Actually, I didn't feel I had a choice. Emma had a firm hold on me. Surrender was my only option. Besides, seeing Lucinda freak out was great fun. Her tail drooped. Her ears twitched. She lay flat against the floor, legs splayed. She looked like a ratty doormat that had seen better days.

Later, after Emma tired of the game, she released us. Lucinda shucked the towel and scurried up her tower. I claimed the sunny patch while Emma set the table.

When Mike called Zach, he didn't answer. Mike slowly climbed the stairs. Partway up, he stopped to catch his breath. "Zach, dinner is ready."

A door opened. Zach appeared. "I heard you," he muttered as he stomped past Mike.

Throughout dinner, Lucinda stationed herself beside Emma's chair, a prime spot for crumbs that might drop to the floor. I settled across the kitchen, far from Zach's swinging legs.

"What's this?" Zach pointed to a platter of hamburgers.

"Go ahead. Help yourself." Mike slid the platter towards him.

Zach shoved the platter back and crossed his arms. "No way. I'm vegetarian."

Mike shrugged. "Really? Sorry, I didn't know. Your mother didn't mention that."

"I'm not surprised. She's more into herself than she is into us."

Mike took a deep breath. "Your mother has a lot to deal with, Zach. She just forgot."

"Yeah, right."

"I can make you something else."

"Don't bother."

Zach reached across the table, grabbed the bowl of fries, and emptied it onto his plate. "I'll make do."

Throughout dinner, Emma chatted constantly. Zach didn't utter another word. To Lucinda's immense pleasure, Emma dropped tasty scraps on the floor. Most she caught before they even landed.

During a lull in Emma's chatter, Mike put down his fork. He cleared his throat. "Zach and Emma. You'll be staying here a while. How long, no one really knows, but it's important that you don't miss school."

Zach locked his eyes on his plate. Emma leaned closer, smiling.

"There's a school a few blocks from here. Tomorrow, we'll go together and enroll both of you."

"Oh, goodie," Emma clapped her hands.

Zach glared at Mike. "Whatever."

He pushed back his chair and dug into his pocket for his cellphone. A smile crept across his lips as he tapped out a message.

Mike gripped the edge of the table. He drew a breath, then reached to take Zach's phone.

Zach tried to pull the phone back. "What are you doing?"

"Sorry, no cellphones at the dinner table."

Zach's face reddened. "You can't do that."

"Yes, I can." Mike placed the phone beside his plate. "This is my home. While you are a guest here, I expect you'll follow my rules."

"Guest?" Zach slammed his fork on the table. "You make it sound like I have a choice. Do you really think I want to be stuck here with you?"

Emma looked at Zach. Then at Mike. Her lip trembled. "Please don't fight."

"We're not fighting." Mike tapped Emma's hand. "We're just having a discussion."

"A discussion?" Zach crossed his arms. "Is that what you call this?"

Mike turned to Zach. "You're right, Zach. You don't have a choice. And I suppose in a way, I don't either. We are family. We are stuck with each other whether we like it or not."

Mike slid Zach's phone across the table. "Take it. It's yours. But please don't bring it to the table again."

Zach grabbed the phone and pushed his chair back.

"Where are you going?" Mike's voice was calm and even. "We're not finished. There's still dessert."

"I don't want any."

"That's your choice, but no one leaves the table until the meal is over."

"Another one of your stupid rules?"

Mike nodded. "Sit down please."

Throughout the rest of the meal, Zach sat in silence, arms crossed, a sneer wrapped across his face.

Chapter 19

Zach disappeared into his room after dinner, slamming the door behind him. After washing the dishes, Mike watched TV. Emma sat on one side of him. I sat on the other.

Jess called to say that she had arrived home safely. "That's a relief," Mike said.

While Mike and Jess talked, Emma manned the remote. She flipped through channels at warp speed. I zoned out, too distracted by Emma to really pay attention to Mike's conversation.

"Let's talk again tomorrow," Mike said, hanging up.

Earlier than usual, Mike escorted Emma upstairs. "School tomorrow," he reminded her.

Emma beamed, but partway up she stopped. She pulled on Mike's hand. "Can Lucy sleep with me tonight?"

"Of course."

In the kitchen, Emma gathered the cat in her arms. Lucinda dug her claws into the carpet of her tower, meowing and hissing, but Emma pried her free.

"Come Lucy. We'll sleep together."

As they mounted the stairs, Lucinda hung limp in Emma's arms as if the bones had been plucked from her body. I followed, one step at a time. When Emma rounded the corner, I caught a glimpse of Lucinda's head bobbing over her shoulder. Her sad eyes were pleading. *Please let me go.*

Mike knocked on Zach's door. "Are you okay? Do you need anything?"

Zach didn't answer. Mike put his hand on the door knob, then took it away. "Good night, Zach. I'm just down the hall. I'll leave my door open in case you need anything."

"Good night, Zach," Emma called.

But there was no answer.

"Maybe he's already asleep," Emma whispered.

"Maybe. Maybe."

In her room, a few steps away from Mike's, Emma settled quickly. She yawned and stretched. When Lucinda wriggled to free herself, Emma pinned her down like one of those wrestlers on TV.

"Grandpa, tell me a story."

I curled up on my blanket at the foot of the bed. A story. My favourite part of the day.

Mike sat on the bed beside her. "Well, let's see." He looked at the ceiling and nodded his head. "Okay. Close your eyes."

"Why?"

"That way you'll be able to picture what I am telling you."

"Oh. Okay." Emma pulled Lucinda closer and closed her eyes. "I'm ready."

"Once upon a time," Mike began.

Emma's head shot up. "So far, I like this story."

Mike chuckled. "That's good. Now close your eyes again."

Mike's voice grew soft, the way it always did when he shared a story. "Once upon a time, long ago, there was a prince and his faithful dog, Svana."

I looked up. I knew this story. As Mike continued, I closed my eyes. I pictured the prince and Svana as they searched for heaven.

"The end," Mike said a little later.

Emma was quiet for a while. "So the prince and his dog are in heaven now?"

"That's how the story goes."

Emma rolled over, squishing Lucinda. "I like that story."

Mike bent down and kissed Emma's forehead. "Good night, sweetheart. If you need anything, I'll be right down the hall."

That night, I dreamed of heaven with its thousands of twinkling stars. I saw Canis Major and its brightest star, Sirius. Was there room for another star up there?

The dream ended when Emma crept into the room, dragging Lucinda with her. "I'm scared, Grandpa."

"There, there," Mike tossed back the covers. "You can sleep here."

For the rest of the night, Emma and Lucinda slept beside Mike. I slept on my blanket on the hard floor. No way was I going to share a bed with a cat, and especially not that one.

Chapter 20

Sun streamed through the curtains as Mike jolted awake. He glanced at the clock, moaned, and tore back the covers.

"Get up, Emma. We've slept in."

Mike hurried to the bathroom. "Go wake up Zach," he called. "We're going to be late if we don't hurry."

Emma yawned and slid off the bed. Lucinda trailed after her, leaving me with a few moments of peace. I'd hardly slept at all.

Down the hall, I heard a knock on a door, then the squeal of hinges needing oil. "Zach, Grandpa says you have to get up."

"Get lost," Zach shouted. The door slammed. "I hate school. I'm not going anywhere."

By the time Mike and I reached Zach's room, the shouting had ended. Emma stood beside the door, whimpering softly. Lucinda was nowhere to be seen.

Mike took Emma by the hand. "Come. Let's get you ready."

He led Emma to her room, spread her clothes on the bed, wiped away her tears, then returned to Zach's door. "Zach, may I come in?"

Zach didn't answer. Mike opened the door and peered into the room. "Zach?"

Socks, underwear, jeans, and t-shirts littered the

floor. Pages from Zach's notepad were strewn about the room. Many were filled with sketches of angry people screaming at each other.

Zach stood at the window in his pyjama bottoms. He ran a hand under his nose and sniffed.

"I'm not going to school."

I wormed my way into Zach's room. Odours wafted from the clothes on the floor—the stench of sweat from an unwashed t-shirt, the stink of feet from a dirty sock. I sniffed around the pile and breathed in all the smells of Zach.

Mike sat on the bed. The springs groaned under the added weight. "I understand," he said in a soft voice. "Change is never easy."

Zach wheeled around. "What would you know about that?"

"I've had a few changes of my own."

"Yeah, well, so what?"

"So that's life. There's no escaping change."

Zach crossed his arms and sneered. "Wow. Talk about obvious."

Mike nodded. "I understand that you're angry. I understand that you're going through a tough time. I'm here to help, if you want it." Mike glanced at me. "We're all here to help."

Zach pointed at me. "We? You mean that runt of a dog? Some help."

"Help comes in many forms," Mike said. "The trick is knowing enough to accept it when it appears."

I was hurt by Zach's remark. If I could speak, I

would have returned his snide comment. *Who are you calling a runt? Have you looked in the mirror lately?*

Without words to use, I did the next best thing. I found Zach's underwear on the floor. I stuffed my nose into the crotch. I inhaled the odours that were his. Then I sank my teeth into the fabric. I chewed and chewed, absorbing the flavours that were all Zach's.

"Here's the thing, Zach." Mike said. He stood up and stepped closer. "I need you to go to school. Emma needs you to go."

Zach laughed. He turned around to gaze out the window. "So you're playing the concerned grandfather now. Nice one. But, no. I'm not going and you can't make me."

Mike drew a deep breath before continuing. "I have an appointment this afternoon. I can't change it and it's going to run late. I need you to make sure that Emma gets home safely."

I looked at Mike. His voice was gravelly. He spoke slowly as if his tongue had trouble forming the words. "Can you do this for me? Can you do it for Emma?"

"What's in it for me?"

"Probably nothing." Mike's face drained of colour. "It's just what families do. We try to help each other."

"Exactly what are my parents doing to help me? They're so busy hating each other, they don't even know I exist."

"You're wro—"

Mike wobbled unsteadily. He sat down on the bed and fished out a bottle of pills from his pocket. His hands shook as he pried it open.

I left Zach's underwear and nudged Mike's leg. He didn't seem to notice.

Zach spun around. "I'm not wrong," he started to say. When he saw the bottle in Mike's hand, his face lost its fierce look. He opened his mouth to say more, then closed it again.

Mike popped a pill into his mouth. Slowly, his hands steadied. His laboured breathing eased. "Can you do this for us, Zach?" he asked again.

Zach blinked. He swallowed and nodded. "Okay. I'll do it." He looked out the window again. "I'll do it for Emma. Just this once."

Mike stuffed the bottle into his pocket. "Thanks, Zach. I knew I could count on you."

As I followed Mike down the stairs, shouts rang from Zach's room. "That stupid dog. I'm going to kill him. Look what he did to my underwear!"

I felt a tiny bit of guilt. Mostly, though, I felt hugely satisfied.

Chapter 21

Even though we were late, our walk to school was slow. Emma marched alongside Mike, who moved carefully, one hand on Emma's shoulder, the other holding my leash. Zach lagged behind, a scowl on his face. I kept ahead of him, far from his reach.

"Stupid dog," he muttered. "That was my favourite pair."

Dampness hung in the chilly air, worsening my arthritis. I was grateful for Mike's slower pace. Along the way, he pointed out features to Zach so he could find his way home. Zach grumbled the occasional "Yeah, I've got it," but otherwise he barely spoke a word.

From my walks with Mike, I knew the route. Two blocks down the street. A right turn at the Asian restaurant. A left at the firehall where the flag fluttered on the pole outside. Another left at the playground.

Mike checked his watch. "School has already started. We'll have to go to the office to register."

He dug into his pocket and pulled out a key. "Zach, do you think you can find your way home?"

Zach rolled his eyes. "Yeah. Of course."

"You'll remember to wait for Emma, won't you?"

Zach shifted his backpack and snatched the key. "I'm not a baby. I said I would and I will."

He grabbed Emma's hand. "Come on. Let's get this ordeal over with."

Mike tied my leash to the bike rack and patted my head. "I'll just be a few minutes, Coop."

It seemed like days. I waited, sprawled on the pavement, eyes locked on the door, expecting Mike at any moment. I began to wonder if maybe Mike had ditched me. It wouldn't be the first time an owner abandoned me.

Finally, I nodded off, so bored I couldn't keep awake any longer.

A bell rang. Still no Mike. I dozed some more, lost in a dream.

Voices woke me up. Recess. Kids everywhere. I dozed some more.

I felt a jab. Two boys stood over me, one tall, the other short, both holding sticks.

"Get-a-load-a this," the short one sneered.

"Whadya suppose it is?"

"I dunno. One of those ugly wiener breeds."

I clambered to my feet, unsteady from my long wait. I backed away as far as the leash allowed. I knew the type. The bullying kind who felt important by making others feel awful about themselves.

The short boy jabbed me with the stick. "Look, he's scared."

I barked. Honestly, I surprised myself.

The boys stepped back, giggling nervously. Then they edged closer, flashing their sticks like sabres.

"What's going on?" a gruff voice said.

Mike.

I barked some more. Not that I needed to, not with Mike casting a huge shadow over the boys. But somehow, it felt important to show Mike that I could speak for myself.

Mike's eyebrows shot up. He put his hands on his hips and widened his stance. "You weren't going to hurt my dog, were you?"

The short boy took a step back. The other gulped and swallowed.

"That's what I thought," Mike said. "Now don't you have better things to do?"

The boys nodded. Without another word, they threw their sticks on the ground and fled.

Mike smiled. He stooped to pat me. "There, there. Nice voice you have there, Coop. Glad to hear you speak up."

He checked his watch as he untied me. "I've lost track of time. We'd better hurry."

At first, we walked briskly. I could barely keep up. But at the Asian restaurant, Mike stopped to catch his breath. "I just need a minute, Coop," he said, leaning against the building.

Mike stopped two more times before we arrived home. Once inside, he popped a pill, slumped onto a chair and held his head in his hands. I sat beside him. Even Lucinda—normally so self-absorbed that she didn't notice such things—leaped from her tower to check on him.

"I'll be all right," Mike wheezed. "I'll be all right."

Chapter 22

Mike left just after lunch. Lucinda lounged on her tower. I lay on my blanket and caught up on sleep lost the night before.

I woke up to the squeal of hinges. Feet pounded the floor. The kitchen door tore open. Emma raced into the room. She flung her backpack onto a chair, patted my head, then charged over to Lucinda.

"Lucy, I missed you."

Emma grabbed the cat in both arms and ran into the hall. I caught a glimpse of Lucinda's sad face as Emma rounded the corner and thumped up the stairs.

I was beginning to feel sorry for Lucinda. There was no place for her to hide, no corner safe from Emma's reach. I relaxed, grateful that I wasn't the target of Emma's smothering affection.

Usually Mike let me outside as soon as he came home. I waited at the back door, but nobody noticed. I yipped, then barked. Still no response.

I heard voices from the living room, then a round of applause. I crept down the hall to check.

Zach lay sprawled on the couch, feet propped up on the coffee table. He held the remote in one hand, a tissue against his mouth with the other. A bruise coloured his swollen cheek. A dark ring circled his right eye. When he pulled the tissue away, it was wet with blood.

I nudged Zach's leg, but his eyes never left the TV. I pawed the sofa. I barked to reinforce the message. *I have to go!*

"What do you want, mutt?" Zach growled, swatting me away with his hand.

I crept to a safe spot, close to the TV, but far from Zach. I didn't trust him. I could feel his anger from across the room.

Several of my many previous owners had anger issues like Zach. One was a sweaty guy with an overhanging belly, nice enough most times except when he was drinking. One day, as he stumbled off the couch, drink in hand, he tripped over me. "Get out of my way, mutt," he screamed. Then he kicked me, sending me flying against the wall.

My blanket held proof of our short relationship—a yellow stain from the glass of whisky that landed on it.

Zach finally settled for a program about space travel on the National Geographic channel. He had never shown an interest in anything except music and sports, so it was a surprising choice. Nestled on my blanket, wedged between a large vase and a side table, I watched, one eye on the TV, the other on Zach.

The program was grainy, but fascinating. Footage of a rocket on a launchpad rolled by. A man with a soothing voice narrated the scene.

"On November 3, 1957, the Soviet Union launched Sputnik 2. It was the first rocket to carry a live animal into space."

A photograph of a dog appeared. "Laika, a crossbreed mongrel, was selected for her even temperament.

She was a stray, found wandering the streets of Moscow."

I perked up. Laika looked a lot like Max from Derby—a Siberian husky-terrier mutt.

The scene changed to fuzzy photos of a cone-shaped capsule and the instruments inside. One photo showed a sealed cabin built just for Laika.

"At the time," the narrator said, "little was known about the effects of space travel on creatures. Sputnik 2 was an experiment designed to see if a living passenger could survive a launch into orbit."

Other photos flashed by. Laika sitting inside the small cabin. Laika wearing a special harness. Laika with wires running from the harness to a panel of instruments.

I crept closer to the TV. Laika looked amazingly calm.

Film footage of the rocket on the launch pad reappeared. Steam boiled below the rocket. It lifted, slowly at first, then faster as it disappeared into the clouds.

The narrator's voice broke in again. "Liftoff took place at 5:30p.m., Moscow time. Sputnik 2 orbited the earth as planned. Data showed that although Laika's heart rate and breathing increased during takeoff, she reached orbit unhurt."

All at once, the channel changed. "Boring and stupid," Zach muttered, punching buttons on the remote.

Laika? What happened to her?

I gave Zach a pleading look. *Go back. Please!*

But Zach settled on another channel. "Now this is more like it."

Two men wearing shorts stood in a ring. A bell rang. The men danced and hammered each other with huge gloves. The bell rang again and the men stopped. Blood dripped from one man's lip. When the bell rang, the two men faced off again. The pounding started all over.

Zach leaned forward, a smile on his face. In the glow of the TV, the circle that rimmed his eye looked darker.

"Finish him off with an uppercut," he screamed.

I had no interest in the sport. Instead, I dozed. But it was a restless sleep. Cramps seized my bowels. I had to go so badly I thought I might burst.

Chapter 23

Unlike humans who can open doors, flush toilets, and take care of their private needs without help, dogs—at least the trained ones—rely on their owners when it comes to waste disposal. We can give hints— bark, jump, squirm. You'd have to be a complete dolt to miss our cues. Or someone who is lazy and just doesn't care. Or someone like Zach who is so preoccupied with himself he didn't even notice.

How long I dozed, I couldn't say. I awoke to Emma standing over her brother. "I'm hungry," she said, tapping his leg.

He pushed her aside to watch TV. "Grandpa will be home soon."

Emma flopped into a chair, crossed her arms, and pursed her lips. "I can't wait that long."

The words ricocheted through my mind. I couldn't wait either. Not just because I was hungry—though I was—but because I had to go so desperately.

I barked and danced around Zach's legs. "Shut up, mutt." He swiped at me with a magazine.

"Zach, don't." Emma reached to tear the magazine away from Zach.

While they fought for control of the magazine, I charged into the kitchen. I barked and pawed at the back door. I couldn't wait. Not a moment longer.

So I went. Right there. I left a huge, smelly mound on the carpet beside the door.

For the rest of the afternoon, I hid under the corner chair, ashamed of my act. Zach and Emma drifted in and out of the kitchen, snatching bits of food that they carried into the living room. No one noticed me or seemed to smell the poop at the door. Not even Lucinda, who stayed as far away from Emma as possible.

Hours later, long past Mike's usual arrival time, I heard the clink of keys at the front door and a weak "I'm home, kids." Heavy feet shuffled down the hallway. Mike staggered into the dark kitchen, huffing. A chemical smell seeped across the room. He flicked on the light. He surveyed the dishes on the counter, the open packages of snacks on the table, and the crumbs that littered the floor.

Mike shook his head. He wandered to Lucinda's tower and stroked her fur. "Quite the mess, Lucy," he sighed. He gazed around the room. "Where's Coop?"

He found me, hunched and hiding in the corner. "What are you doing there?" He stooped, joints creaking, to reach me. "Come, Coop."

But I burrowed deeper into the corner, embarrassed and fearing the worst: Derby. No doubt Mike would turn me in once he discovered what I'd done.

Mike beckoned with his finger. "What's wrong, Coop?" He straightened up, then turned towards the door. "Come, let's go outside."

But I wouldn't. I just wanted to melt into the floor.

Mike shuffled across the kitchen. I heard him sigh. I heard him mutter curse words I can't repeat.

"What's this? Zach! Come here. Emma, you too."

Zach rounded the corner, followed by his sister. I crept out from my hiding place, too curious to stay away.

"Look at this," Mike pointed to the mound. "Didn't you let Coop out when you came home?"

He started to say something more but stopped. He stepped towards Zach and reached to touch his face. "What happened to you?"

Zach brushed his hand away. "It's nothing."

"He was in a fight," Emma said.

Zach curled his fingers into a fist. "Shut up, Em."

Emma backed away. Tears flooded her eyes.

"Were you, Zach?" Mike asked.

"Yeah, so what? You should have seen the other guy." Zach wheeled around, flung open the door, and stormed outside. "Just leave me alone, will you."

The kitchen filled with silence. Mike shook his head. He sat down, gripping the edges of the table as he eased himself onto the chair. He wiped a bead of sweat off his brow and drew Emma closer.

"I didn't mean to get Zach in trouble," she sobbed.

Mike wiped away Emma's tears. "He's just upset with himself. He'll come around. He just needs time."

Later, Mike let me outside. I found Zach sitting on the bench in the dark, sobbing.

"It's not fair. It just isn't."

When Mike let me in again, the smell of disinfectant

lingered in the air. A pail of soapy water stood near the door. A sponge floated inside. I sidestepped the wet patch, not daring to look at Mike.

"There, there." he said. "It's okay, Coop. It wasn't your fault."

When Zach entered later, he sidestepped the wet patch, too. He kept his head down and didn't make eye contact with Mike either.

Zach didn't say anything. But then again, neither did Mike.

Dinner was a hurried and tense affair. Zach played with his food and didn't utter a word. Mike seemed lost in his thoughts. Only Emma spoke. She rattled on about her new teacher and the friends she'd made at school.

Afterwards, Zach disappeared into this room, only re-emerging once to use the bathroom. Mike moved slowly and stopped several times on the way up the stairs. He read a story to Emma and tucked her in. He stood outside Zach's door, his hand on the door-knob, then shook his head and went into his own room instead.

That evening, in the middle of a story from *Everything Dogs*, the phone rang.

"Jess, is this you?" Mike said.

A frown wrinkled his brow. "Who is this?"

I edged closer, ears perked to hear better.

"Who is this?" Mike said again.

A growly voice sifted through the phone's speaker.

Mike threw back the covers and swung his legs off the bed. "Rick?"

I crept to the edge of the mattress as Mike paced the floor. Furrows on his brow deepened as he listened. "Rick. They're not here, understand."

Mike said a few more things. So did Rick. Although Mike spoke calmly, his voice trembled. "Don't call again, Rick," he said before slamming down the receiver to end the call.

Mike slipped back into bed, huffing. He looked at Eva and shook his head. "I lied, my dear. What else could I do?"

That night, I snuggled close to Mike, my head pressed against his heaving chest. I fell asleep listening to the unsteady beats of his heart and the long pauses in between.

Chapter 24

Over the next few days, we established new routines. On weekdays, Zach and Emma went to school and returned together. Usually, Mike was home by then with dinner almost ready. If Mike was away, Emma let me outside. Zach, meanwhile, flopped on the couch to watch TV.

I learned to read Zach's mood by the way he handled the remote. If he was angry, he flicked from channel to channel and rarely spent more than a few seconds on any program. If he watched anything at all, it was usually one of those combat shows where spectators yelled and screamed as two people pounded each other.

On those days, I steered clear of Zach.

Jess called each evening. She always asked to speak to the kids. Emma came to the phone, eager to share the highlights from her day. Not Zach, though. He refused to talk to Jess. He spent evenings in his room with the door closed.

Mike never mentioned Rick's phone call to Jess, but I learned a few things from what he did say to her. For one, Rick was a bigger pain than ever. He phoned Jess several times a day. He asked to speak with Zach and Emma and cursed and threatened Jess when they didn't come to the phone. If Jess mentioned the support

"Yeah. Me, too."

Zach roamed the kitchen, inspecting cupboards. "Not a thing. Unless you want cereal. Even then, there's no milk in the fridge."

Suddenly, he stopped. "Wait a minute."

He opened the cookie jar and drew out a handful of coins and a few bills. "Let's go get something. There's a 7-Eleven a few blocks from here."

Emma hesitated. "Are you sure?"

But Zach was already at the door, keys in one hand and money in the other.

Emma released Lucinda. The cat bounded up the tower, snug sweater and all. I circled Emma as she put on her jacket. After a long day in the stuffy house, I needed a break, too.

"Coop wants to go." Emma said.

"Come on. Speed it up."

We walked briskly down the sidewalk. Emma held my leash. Zach led the charge. A quiet breeze sifted through trees, filling the street with the smell of blossoms. It was a wonderful June evening. Had I not been so worried about Mike, I might have enjoyed it more. Where was he? Why wasn't he home yet?

Zach took two steps for every one of Emma's. She ran to keep up, tugging the leash to hurry me along. My legs churned. Down the street we ran, past familiar houses and yards.

"Slow down," Emma pleaded.

We stormed down one street, then another, and then still another. A block later, Zach crossed an intersection. We weaved down a maze of lanes and alleys. We passed buildings I didn't recognize. Finally, we reached a busy highway.

"Let's see," Zach said. "It's got to be here somewhere."

Cars streamed by. Their headlights pierced the growing darkness. Across the highway, neon lights blazed, each one advertising a service.

"Where are we?" Emma was out of breath. Amid the rush of traffic, her voice sounded tiny and scared.

Like Emma, I was out of breath. *Yes, where were we?* I'd never been this way before.

A semi thundered past, raining gravel and dust on us. "We have to be close," Zach said. He peered down the highway, gazing left and right.

"I thought you knew where we were going!"

"We must have made a wrong turn somewhere." Zach stuffed his hands in his pockets and shrugged. "Come on. Let's go back."

"I can't," Emma sobbed. "I'm too tired and hungry."

"You can do it, Em." Zach said softly. "We'll stop to rest whenever you want. It's not that far. We'll find our way. You'll see."

Zach was lying. We were definitely lost.

Chapter 25

Darkness swallowed us. Traffic roared by.
"I'm scared," Emma sniffled.

"I know."

This was a different Zach. Not the pouting, surly Zach of an hour ago. A tender Zach. I nudged his leg. Like Emma, I was scared, too.

"Get away, mutt," Zach said, pushing me away.

Okay, not so different.

"Come, Em." Zach took his sister's hand. Emma tugged the leash gently, encouraging me to follow. We walked along the shoulder of the busy highway, retracing our steps. Down the street that led to the highway. Down the one after that.

Streetlights cast eerie shadows. Buildings looked as if they'd been washed in coats of grey and black. None of the landmarks looked familiar.

"My feet hurt," Emma whined.

Mine did, too. Pain shot through my pads and seeped into my delicate joints. Every muscle ached.

"Not much farther, Em. It's just around the corner."

Another one of Zach's lies as it turned out. The next street was as foreign and empty as all the others. "Must be the next one then," he said lamely.

Emma pulled her hand free from Zach's. She stopped dead. A giant tear rolled down her cheek. "You don't know where we are, do you?"

Zach peered down the street, scanning houses that all looked the same. "I wish I'd brought my phone."

When a car veered around the corner, Zach stepped into the street and waved his arms. Maybe the driver didn't see Zach. Maybe he didn't care. He plowed on, leaving us alone. The hum of highway traffic was only a distant memory now.

Emma sobbed. Zach stepped ahead, hesitated, then stepped back. In his eyes, I saw doubt and uncertainty. Maybe even a bit of fear.

I wondered if Mike had come home. Surely, he would look for us. Surely, he'd be worried.

Above Emma's sobs, I heard a faint sound carried by the wind. The ting of metal striking metal. I turned to Zach and Emma. Did they hear it, too? But Zach merely stared at the ground, kicking stones at his feet.

Ting. Ting. It was a familiar sound. Where had I heard it before?

Of course. The fire hall. The fluttering flag. The clips holding it striking the metal mast. That was their sound.

I barked and tugged on the leash, almost toppling Emma.

"Shut up, mutt," Zach yelled.

I danced around Emma, barking louder. I tugged some more, harder this time, so hard the leash slipped from her hand.

"Coop!" Emma squealed.

Free, I charged ahead, yipping. A few houses away, I glanced back. Emma was running a few steps behind me, flinging her arms and wailing. "Coop! Come back!"

Zach loped after her. "Em! Wait up!"

The tinging sound grew louder with each step. Out of breath, I rounded a corner and stopped under a streetlight. Ahead, the unfurled flag at the firehall fluttered in the breeze. *Ting, ting*, the clips sang with each strike against the mast.

Seconds later, Emma and Zach caught up, huffing and wheezing.

"You stupid dog," Zach snarled.

He swung his leg to kick me, but Emma stepped in to stop him.

"Zach. Don't," she screamed.

Zach clenched his fists. He dropped his arms to his side. "Dumb mutt."

He grabbed the leash, yanked me hard, and turned to cross the street. "Come on, Em. It's this way."

I dug my paws into the pavement. I barked again, more insistent now. *Look.*

Emma was the first to notice. "Zach!" She pointed down the street to a large building under a row of lights on the edge of a playground.

Zach scratched his head. "Well, what do you know. The school." He glanced at me. "Guess the dog's not as stupid as I thought."

Coming from Zach, this was a compliment.

"See," Emma grabbed the leash. "I told you he was smart."

I barked, eager for more praise.

"Shut up, mutt," Zach said.

Chapter 26

Home beckoned. I led the way even though I didn't have to. I ignored the pain in my legs and the thirst that left my tongue paper dry. I pressed on, past the Asian restaurant, down the street with the lopsided house, down the one with the giant evergreen. I tugged Emma while Zach lingered behind, dragging his feet. Coins jingled in his pockets. Coins from Mike's cookie jar.

Worry drove me towards home. Worry about Mike. Worry that he would be worried.

I knew worry. Worry had been my companion my whole life. Mostly I worried about myself. How long would it be before my owners grew tired of me? Would they drop me off along some deserted road? Or would they take me to a shelter and leave me behind again?

This was a different kind of worry. Not worry about myself. Worry about Mike. He wasn't well. It didn't take a genius to figure that out. His shortness of breath. The way he clutched the railing as he climbed the stairs. The pills he popped more and more often now. It was all getting worse.

If I needed more proof, there was also the phone conversation I overheard one day. "Doctor Poon." Mike said then, "Sorry, but I can't come to the hospital for my appointment today. Can we reschedule?"

My head shot up when I heard that. *Hospital?* I worried even more about Mike after that.

Light streamed from the windows of the house as we turned into the yard. I bounded up the steps, barking madly. Emma followed, breathless but excited. Zach pulled up his hoodie, stuffed his hands in his pockets and hung back.

The door opened. Mike stepped out. He looked awful—pasty white, eyes sunken, legs wobbly. A smile broke across his face when he saw us.

"Thank goodness," he said, reaching to hug Emma. I danced around his legs and yipped, while Zach stared at the houses across the street.

"Come in. Come in." Mike waved us inside.

That night, I lapped water until my bowl was empty. I ate every scrap of food Mike fed me. Then I lay on my blanket to watch and listen as Mike and the kids downed a hurried meal of toast and scrambled eggs. Lucinda settled beside Emma's chair, purring contentedly. Maybe it was my imagination, but I think she had missed us, too.

Mike didn't ask many questions. He didn't have to. Emma chatted the whole time, describing everything in detail. How we'd gone searching for the 7-Eleven. How we'd gotten lost. How we found our way home again.

"We might have wandered forever if it hadn't been for Coop," she said, dropping a morsel of egg on the floor.

"Well done, Coop." Mike said.

I nudged Mike's leg. It felt good to be the hero for a change.

Emma left out a few details that Mike seemed to notice. When the meal was over, he turned to Zach.

"Do you have anything to add? Anything you want to say?"

Zach shook his head. "I think Emma pretty much covered it."

Mike nodded. "I see. Well, you were in charge, right? This was your idea."

"Yeah," Zach's voice was so low, I could barely hear him.

"And?"

"And I guess it wasn't the best idea."

"And?"

Zach gripped the table and leaned back. "I guess I should have left a note."

"And?"

"And nothing. What do you want me to say? It was a stupid idea. I get it."

Mike nodded. "Yes, it was. But there is something else." He grabbed the cookie jar off the counter. "The lid was off. I wondered why."

Zach stared at his plate, not uttering a word.

Mike placed the jar on the table in front of Zach.

"So I took a few coins," Zach pushed his chair back. "It's not like I robbed a bank."

"And that makes it okay?"

Zach squirmed. "You weren't around to ask and there wasn't anything here to eat, thanks to you. When was the last time, you bought groceries anyways?" Zach pushed back his chair. "All you think about is yourself."

"I'm sorry," Mike sputtered. "I guess...I guess I forgot"

Zach reached into his pocket, pulled out a fistful of coins and bills, and slammed them on the table. "Here. Take your stupid money."

He stood up, toppling his chair in his hurry.

"Zach, please sit…"

Mike's face paled. He winced, clutched his chest, and pointed to the bottle on the counter. "My pills."

Zach stood frozen like one of the statues outside. "How many?" he asked finally.

"Just one."

Zach passed the pill to Mike. "How often does this happen?"

"Not often," Mike lied.

Slowly Mike's wheezing eased. Colour returned to his cheeks.

That evening, while Mike and Emma rested on the couch, Zach cleared dishes off the table and washed them. Later, he escorted Mike upstairs and made sure he was settled. He read a story to Emma and tucked her into bed. Then he checked the house, locking doors and shutting off lights. To my surprise, he even patted my head.

"You may be ugly," he said. "But I guess you weren't the stupidest one today."

Chapter 27

A week after the 7-Eleven incident, Jess showed up. She held a string of balloons in one hand, in the other, a large box.

Emma raced to the door. "Are those for me?"

Jess grinned. "Now what makes you think that?"

Emma planted her hands on her hips. "You know why. It's my birthday!"

We all knew it was Emma's birthday. She'd been preparing for it for days. She'd decorated the kitchen with streamers. She covered the table with a paper tablecloth that Mike bought at the dollar store. She set the table with colourful paper plates. She made little name tags for each of her guests. She even made party hats for everyone, Lucinda and me included.

At the party, Mike and Jess wore their hats. Zach refused to put on his. I tore mine off ten minutes after Emma strapped it to my head. But Lucinda couldn't get hers off. It was fastened with tape and elastic bands.

While I watched from under my chair, six giggling girls from Emma's class raced around the kitchen chasing Lucinda. The poor cat ran laps around the table to dodge their eager hands. Finally, Lucinda dashed under my chair to join me. She wasn't quite quick enough. Or thin enough. Her rear half stuck out. Her tail was like a handle for enthusiastic hands to pull. One of the girls nabbed it and hauled her out.

"I just love her," the girl cooed. She hugged the cat so tight I thought Lucinda might explode.

Most of the time, I stayed under the chair. For reasons I didn't understand, I felt uneasy. Something awful was about to happen. I could feel it in my gut.

For much of the party, Lucinda was the star. Zach hid in his room. Mike hovered in the background, a weary smile on his face. Jess took charge and organized a few party games to bring order to the chaos.

After a few games, she clapped her hands. "Take a seat everyone."

The girls grabbed chairs and sat at the table. Lucinda fled to the middle of the kitchen, close enough to nab bits that might drop to the floor, but safe from grabbing hands.

"Zach," Jess yelled. "Join us please."

Zach slipped into the kitchen. He stood by the door, hands in his pockets, eyes rolling. Mike stationed himself beside the table, camera in hand. Jess busied herself at the counter.

"Ready, everyone?" Jess said. "All together now."

She carried a large, round cake topped with thick frosting and blazing candles. As Jess steered across the kitchen, voices broke into song.

Happy birthday to you. Happy birthday to you.

I froze. There was something familiar about this scene. I'd been through this before. A birthday. Voices singing. Candles blazing.

A long-hidden memory came to life. A different time and place. Another cake with flickering candles. Another family celebrating. And me. I saw myself, too, sprawled on my blanket in the centre of the kitchen.

A tall woman carried the cake. She walked slowly—like Jess—careful not to blow out the candles. She didn't see me below her feet.

I had buried the memory so deep, I'd almost forgotten it. But now, it played in my head in colourful detail. I saw the tall woman nearing me. I felt her foot strike my side. I saw the cake fly, flinging candles onto the table. I saw the paper tablecloth ignite and the flames spread quickly. I heard the screams of children and a woman shouting orders. I felt the pain of flesh burning as embers landed on me. And I smelled the horrible stench that comes from fur that is burning.

I remembered it all.

All at once, the scene in my mind dissolved. Another took its place. This one was real. Excited children in Mike's kitchen singing, "Happy birthday dear Emma. Happy birthday to you." Jess carrying the cake, candles afire. Lucinda lounging on the floor directly in her way.

I tore out from under the chair. I woofed and ran circles around Jess. *Watch out!*

The children stopped singing. Lucinda hissed. Jess stood still, her eyebrows raised. "What the...?" she said.

She shook her head and took another step.

I woofed at Lucinda. *Get out of the way!*

She arched her back and stared at me. She didn't move.

My heart pounded faster. Flames. Heat. It all felt so real.

"Coop!" Mike put down the camera and reached for me. "What's wrong?"

I dodged him and lunged at Lucinda. I nipped her belly with my teeth, not to hurt her, but to show her I meant business.

Move. Now!

Lucinda snarled. She swiped and grazed my side with her claws. I nipped her again. This time I tasted fur.

From the corner of my eye, I saw Zach move closer. He bent to grab me.

I lunged at him, too.

"The mutt's crazy," he yelled, jumping back.

Lucinda seized the moment to escape. In a single bound, she scaled the cat tower to its highest point. I stood guard underneath and barked some more. *Stay there, Lucinda!!*

Jess stood still in the centre of the kitchen, cake in hand.

"What's going on?" Emma asked.

"That dog is crazy," one of the kids said.

Zach stepped out of the doorway. "Yeah, the dog is nuts. You should get rid of him."

Mike scooped me up in his giant hand. "There, there. Pay him no mind, Coop."

For the rest of the party, I sat in Mike's lap, trembling. He held me close and ran his hand across my back. He whispered soothing words. "There, there. It's okay, Coop. That's all in the past now."

I was confused by Mike's words. How could he possibly know what I was going through when I didn't know myself?

Chapter 28

Later, after Emma's guests had left, Jess called everyone to the table. Mike held me in his arms, gently stroking my back as he took a chair between Zach and Emma. He hadn't let go of me once since the incident.

Zach shuffled to the side, putting distance between the two of us. Now and then, he muttered under his breath and glared at me. I heard only bits of what he said. *Freaking stupid…weirdo…runt…*

Jess cleared her throat and drew a deep breath. "There's something we need to discuss."

She fiddled with a paper napkin as she spoke. "You know that things are not going well between your father and me."

Zach folded his arms across his chest. "No kidding."

Jess reached out to touch his hand, then reconsidered. "It's only become worse lately. Frankly, I'm scared. Scared for myself, but also scared for you."

A tear welled in Emma's eye.

"I know that both of you have been through a lot," Jess said. "Your grandfather has been very helpful, but this is only a temporary situation. We need to find a more permanent solution."

Zach stared ahead, avoiding eye contact. Jess leaned back in her chair and cleared her throat again.

"I don't know how to break the news gently, so I'm just going to say it outright. We're moving to Madison."

Zach's eyes widened. He clenched the table and shoved back his chair. "Madison? That godforsaken place. It's in the middle of nowhere."

Emma turned to Jess. "What's Madison?"

"Madison is a nice town." Mike said. "You'll like it there."

Jess spread a map on the table. She pointed to a dot. "Here's where we are now." She traced her finger along a twisted line. "There's Madison. It's surrounded by mountains and beautiful lakes. It's a wonderful place."

Zach leaned back in his chair. "Sure it is."

"I've found a job there. It pays more than my current one and I can start right away. And I've found us a farmhouse to rent just outside of town. It needs some fixing, but it will do for now."

Jess spread a few photographs on the table. I craned my neck for a better view.

"There's a barn on the property and a huge garden." Jess pointed to the photos as her voice rose. "There are chickens, pigs, even two horses."

"Horses?" Emma leaned in for a closer look.

"Yeah, right." Zach snarled, shooting spit across the table. "Now we're going to be farmers."

Jess looked at Zach. "It will give us a fresh start. We need that. *All* of us need that." She folded the map and tucked it into her purse along with the photos. "Your father won't know where we are. I'll make sure of that."

Zach stood up, toppling the chair. "Did you even consider what this means for us? Moving to a strange town. Another new school where we won't know anyone."

"I've given it a lot of thought," Jess answered calmly.

But Zach was already stomping across the kitchen, halfway to the back door. "You just don't get it, do you?"

He flung open the door. It slammed shut behind him.

No one spoke. Jess fiddled with the napkin. Mike stroked my fur. Emma gazed across the table, a dreamy smile on her lips.

"That went well," Jess said with a sigh.

"He'll come around. He needs time."

"I'll miss my friends," Emma said. Then she brightened. "Horses. Are there really horses there?"

Jess laughed. "I can see you'll have no trouble adjusting. As soon as I can finalize a few things, we'll move."

While Emma played with her birthday gifts, Mike washed dishes. Jess dried. I sprawled at their feet, zoning in and out of their conversation, but mostly rehashing my earlier reaction. Why had I gone so completely nuts? I'd buried the memory of the fire so deep that I'd pretty much forgotten it.

But there was no forgetting now.

I played the memory again. This time I saw things I'd missed before. The tall woman grabbing a fire extinguisher and dousing the flames. A boy stamping on my blanket, putting out the fire. A girl cradling me in her arms. "You'll be okay, Cooper." And then, a man rushing me to the vet to have my burn treated.

Suddenly, the fog around another memory lifted. This time I saw Ruth. I saw the same man, only he was dressed in different clothes. "We have to move," I heard him say to Ruth. "We'd love to take Cooper with us, but we can't. It wouldn't be fair to him. Can you find Cooper a good home?"

The man passed the leash to Ruth. He ruffled my fur, patted my head, then he was gone.

Slowly, the missing pieces of my past fell into place. The fire wasn't really my fault. It was just an accident, plain and simple. I was left at Derby not because my family didn't care for me, but because they did.

After the dishes were cleaned and the kitchen restored to its usual order, Mike and Jess sat at the table.

"I should go check on Zach," Jess said.

"He'll come in when he's ready. Give him time."

Jess nodded. "I guess. It's a big step for him. For all of us."

"You know it's the right thing to do, Jess."

"I suppose. Rick would do anything to get hold of the kids. He's angry. He wants to punish me, to hurt me in the most painful way. He'd make sure I never saw Zach or Emma again."

Mike put his hand on hers. "We're not going to let that happen."

Jess glanced at Emma. "It's a lot to ask of the kids."

"Kids are tougher than they seem. They'll cope. Probably better than you."

Jess left shortly after. When Mike let me out later, I found Zach sitting on the bench, head cupped in his hands. I skirted around him to inspect my territory. Now and then, I heard him sob.

After my rounds, I found my usual place between the flowerpots near the pond. The dog statue that looked like me shimmered in the moonlight. The globe figures hugged each other as if trying to keep warm. Four happy people. Just like my last family.

I felt sorry for Zach. I knew what it was like to start fresh, to leave what was once home and move to another. But I also knew anger and I wanted no part of it.

Chapter 29

Over the next few days, Zach's mood varied. Sometimes he seemed to accept the move. Mostly though, he grumbled. He complained about school. He grouched about meals. He whined about everything.

Emma, on the other hand, wore a constant smile. She spent every spare minute browsing on Mike's computer, researching what horses ate and how they should be handled.

Every evening, Jess phoned. Zach still refused to talk to her, but Emma gleefully shared what she had learned with her mom. Mostly, though, Jess spoke with Mike. She'd found a renter for their current house. She'd booked a moving company to haul their possessions to Madison. In a few days, she would be there, unpacking, settling in, starting a new job, beginning a new life. She'd come for the kids after school ended for the summer.

"Rick doesn't know, does he?" Mike asked her one evening.

As he listened, blood drained from his face. He tore off his glasses and stood up. He closed his eyes and opened his mouth without uttering a word.

"He did that?" he finally said. "Rick smashed the windshield of your car?"

The more Mike talked, the more agitated he

became. "He followed you to work? He broke into the house? You have to leave, Jess. Right now, you hear?"

He walked in tight, nervous circles. "Leave. The sooner, the better. Tomorrow, if you can."

That night, like so many others, I tossed and turned. I liked Emma. I even liked Zach—sometimes anyways. I'd miss them.

And then there was Mike. I worried the most about him. He'd lost weight. His clothes hung in baggy folds on his thin frame. He had to rest often, and he was short-winded much of the time.

That night, just after the clock chimed two, the phone rang.

"Not again," Mike said, jolting awake. "It better not be...."

But it was. It was Rick.

An angry voice seeped through the phone, so loud I could hear Rick's screams and curses myself.

Mike clenched his fist. "I told you before: Zach and Emma are not here."

Mike slammed the receiver down. He stared at Eva's picture and shook his head. "That man! What are we going to do, my dear?"

Mike slept in fits and starts. He fluffed up his pillows and sighed often. He paced the floor, then climbed into bed again. He kept me awake for the rest of the night.

Chapter 30

Over the next few days, Mike kept a close watch on the kids. He walked them to and from school even though Zach complained bitterly.

"I'm not a baby. Do you know how embarrassing this is?"

Mike also peered out windows more often, checked locks on doors, and doubled his rounds about the house each evening before going to bed.

Then, one evening, just as I was getting comfy on the couch to watch a hockey game with Mike, the phone rang. Mike hesitated a moment before picking it up.

"Hello."

A small smile crept across his face as he listened. "Already? That is good news, Jess. I'm glad you are in a safe place now."

I studied his face for clues and listened carefully. Jess, I gathered, had moved to Madison already, sooner than she originally planned. I could feel Mike's relief. The worry left him like air released from a balloon.

"Take your time. Get settled first. The kids are fine here. Besides, they have a few more weeks of school before summer break. We'll come after that."

That night, we both slept better, free of worries, curled beside each other on Mike's bed.

Then, morning came.

A loud buzzer jarred me awake. It sounded again. And again.

Mike rolled over and checked the clock beside the bed. "Only six," he groaned.

Muttering, he tossed the blankets aside. "All right, all right. I'm coming."

Heavy fists pounded on the front door.

"I said I was coming," Mike yelled.

Slippers slapped his heels as Mike shuffled down the hall. He closed Emma's door and then Zach's on the way. I followed him as he thumped down the stairs.

"Come on, Mike. Open up," a man shouted. He pounded the door again.

Mike grabbed the railing. His face drooped. His voice trembled. "What do you want, Rick?"

Mike hobbled to the door, checked the lock, and peered through the peephole. I ran to the front window to see Rick for myself. A bearded man with a ponytail wearing a snug t-shirt stood outside. Tattoos ringed his bulging arms. A silver earring dangled from one ear. He was even taller than Mike, twice his weight, and probably half his age. Behind him, a sporty convertible sat on the driveway.

Rick ran a hand through his beard. He pounded the door again. "Come on, Mike. Let me in."

"Go away, Rick."

Rick stepped back. "They're here, aren't they?"

Mike leaned against the door frame. "You'd better leave or I'll call the police."

"I'm not leaving without them." Rick punched the door with both fists. "Open up, old man."

I climbed the sofa and peered above the arm. I growled, then barked.

Rick's eyes wandered to the window. He laughed. "Some guard dog you have there, Mike."

"Go away, Rick. I mean it. You have a restraining order. You're not supposed to be anywhere near the kids."

Rick shrugged. "I don't care what any judge says. They're my kids, too." He kicked the door. "I know they're here, old man."

Rick slammed his body against the door, rattling pictures that hung on the wall.

"Is that my dad?" a small quivering voice asked.

Emma. Standing at the top of the stairs, hugging Lucinda, eyes wide with concern.

Mike put his fingers to his lips. "Shh. If we're quiet, he'll go away."

"But I want to see him." Emma took a step down the stairs.

Zach appeared behind Emma. "No, you don't." He wrapped an arm around her, pulled her back, and looked into her eyes. "No, *we* don't."

"But I do."

"No, Em. We can't."

Rick swaggered across the driveway, fists knotted into tight balls. "I'll be back. You can bet on it. And next time, I'll bring more than just my fists."

Rick thumped Mike's car, denting the hood. Then

he pulled out his keys and ran them across the driver's door, scraping away a line of paint.

"Just a little reminder in case you forget," he shouted.

He pumped his fist in the air to reinforce the threat. Then he slid behind the wheel of his car. The door slammed, the engine roared. Rick sped out of the driveway, leaving black streaks on the cracked pavement.

Emma sobbed. She tore free from Zach's arms and ran back to her room.

Zach charged down the stairs and stomped down the hall.

"Zach," Mike said. "Wait."

"Screw you," Zach yelled over his shoulder. "Screw everyone."

The back door swung open, then slammed shut, leaving the house in eerie quiet.

Chapter 31

Mike phoned Jess.

"Rick was here. I expect he'll be back."

His voice was tight, stretched like the skin on a drum. He walked in a circle and wove a path around the kitchen table as he filled in the details of Rick's visit. How Rick was convinced the kids were there. How angry he became. How he said he would return, promising worse.

"We have to leave. It's not safe to stay."

He scratched his head. "No, I understand. You're just starting a new job, Jess. You can't pick them up."

He cleared his throat. "We'll leave first thing this afternoon."

After he hung up, Mike climbed the stairs, stopping to catch his breath once. I arrived at the top on the heels of Mike. Both of us were wheezing.

Mike found Emma on her bed, sobbing. He sat beside her and rubbed her shoulders gently.

"I really wanted to see my dad," she said between sniffles.

"Emma, I have some good news. You know those horses you've been talking about?"

Emma looked up. "Yes."

"We're going to see them."

Emma wiped away the tears with the back of her hand. "We are?"

In an instant, she was buzzing around the room, packing up books, sorting through clothes. For the moment, Rick was forgotten.

Mike smiled. "I thought you'd be pleased."

Later, Mike and I went outside. I ran off to refresh my markers as Mike strode down the brick path. His left foot lagged behind his right and it made a scritch-scratch sound as he walked.

After I finished, I joined Mike at the bench where Zach sat. Mike didn't say anything, but Zach seemed to know he was there.

"I hate him," Zach said.

"I understand," Mike said quietly.

"No, you don't. How could you?"

"Do you mind if I sit down?"

"Suit yourself." Zach slid over to the end of the bench. "It's your place, isn't it?"

Mike nodded. The bench sagged as he eased his body down. He folded his hands across his lap and gazed at the globe.

"My parents fought all the time," Mike said.

Zach looked at Mike. "That must have been a long time ago."

Mike smiled. "It was. But some things stay with you your whole life."

Zach started to say something, then didn't.

Mike cleared his throat. "My father had a fiery temper and my mother had a sharp tongue. They argued all the time. Sometimes I got caught in the middle and they would take it out on me. Once...." Mike studied his hands and shook his head.

"Once what?"

"When I was twelve years old, they had a wild fight. My father struck my mother with his fist, then he went after me. I ran as fast as I could, but he was faster and stronger. He nabbed me and started pounding me, then…" Mike drew a deep breath. His voice dropped in pitch. "Then, my mother stepped in. I suppose she was trying to protect me, to surprise my father and give me time to get away. But…"

Mike turned to Zach. "Maybe she was just trying to get even with him. I'm not really sure."

"What happened?" Zach slid a little closer.

"My mother pulled a pot of soup off the stove. She threw it at him." Mike bit his lip. "Only it missed the target."

"What do you mean?"

Mike opened the buttons of his shirt. "It hit me instead."

Zach turned to look. He gasped. I wriggled closer, anxious for a peek too. A band of dark skin, thick and broad, ran across Mike's chest. It looked like the burn patch on my hindquarters, only bigger and deeper.

"Of course, my parents regretted it immediately, but the damage was done."

Zach shifted uncomfortably and looked away. So did I.

Mike buttoned his shirt. "I know. It looks awful. I spent weeks in the hospital and had multiple skin grafts. Things fell apart after that. My father blamed my mother. My mother blamed my father. They split soon after. I was put in a foster home. My brother was placed in another. Eventually, we moved in with our aunt, but life was never the same for any of us."

"You must have been pissed."

"I was. I carried the anger for a long time."

"You don't seem angry now."

Mike smiled. "I'm a different person now. It didn't happen overnight. It took a long time. And I needed help. I still do." His hand dropped to his side. He caressed my ears, lingering over the silky ends. "I didn't want to be like my father. I didn't want to take out my anger on others. I still have bad days, though, days when I would like to punch a hole in the wall."

"But you don't?"

"I've learned to cope."

"Why are you telling me this?"

Exactly my question. What was Mike's point?

Mike placed a hand on Zach's shoulder. "You'll figure it out."

Zach swiped Mike's hand away. "That's no help,"

"Think about it. Give it a little time. We can talk again later if you like."

Mike leaned forward to stand up, then changed his mind. "Perhaps you've heard this saying, Zach. It goes like this. When life gives you sour lemons, find some way to make lemonade."

"That really sucks," Zach grumbled. "What is that supposed to mean anyways?"

"You'll figure it out."

A small smile appeared on Zach's lips. "You're really not very good at this, are you?"

"I'm a little out of practice." Mike patted Zach's shoulder.

The bench groaned as Mike stood. "I've talked to your mother. We think it's best that you and your sister join her in Madison now rather than waiting until school is over."

"Because my dad's a jerk." Zach pounded his fist into his hand.

"Because it's not safe for you to stay. Not for your sister or you. Not for me, either."

"Whatever. Nobody cares what I think anyways." Then Zach said other words that I probably should not repeat.

Mike looked at Zach, then at me. He smiled and nodded.

"We'll be leaving soon. Better get ready, Zach."

Mike shuffled back to the house. A warm breeze swept across the yard, promising another day of blistering heat. I didn't think Zach knew I was there, but as I turned to leave, his hand fell to his side. His fingers grazed my ears. They swept along my back, then gently returned to my head.

"Stupid mutt," Zach growled.

I pressed my snout into his hand. He didn't pull it away. He didn't even flinch when I sniffed his crotch.

Chapter 32

When Zach went inside, I padded behind. Emma stood by the front door, her pink suitcase stuffed to the breaking point.

"I'm ready," she announced.

Zach mounted the stairs without a word while Mike lugged a cooler to the car. He put Emma's suitcase inside the trunk, too.

"Come on, Zach. Hurry! It's a long drive."

Mike made two more trips, once to fetch another suitcase. "Mine." he said to Emma as he added it to the cargo in the trunk.

Her eyebrows shot up.

"It will take two days to get there," he explained. "Another two to return. And I plan on staying a few days to help your mother get settled." He smiled. "Of course, I'll want to check out those horses of yours, too."

Emma clapped her hands and beamed. My heart sank, heavy with dread. Mike. Gone for days. Would he leave me alone? Or worse yet, with Lucinda? Or would he drop me off at Derby?

On his second trip, Mike hauled the kennel to the car and stuffed it into the back seat beside Emma. I grew more nervous. Lucinda? Was she going? What about me?

Zach finally appeared, a backpack flung over his shoulder, earbuds screwed into his ears, and a cellphone in his hand. "Yeah. Yeah. I'm here."

His eyes widened when he saw the kennel. "You're not taking the beasts, are you?"

"I can't leave them here. They can't be left alone that long."

I relaxed.

Mike squeezed Lucinda into the kennel. She whined and clawed as he closed the wire door. "Lucy, you know it's better this way."

Mike turned to Zach. "Coop will be fine if he sits up front, but Lucy has a history of motion sickness. Twists and turns bring out the worst in her."

"Oh, great. Just what I need."

"I've given her some medication to help, but it might take a while to kick in."

By the time we set off, it was already noon. Mike and I sat in the front, a map open on the console between us, his cellphone within reach, a cushion beneath me, and the window open just a crack. Zach and Emma sat in the back with the kennel between them.

We steered down familiar streets, past the school, past the firehouse and Asian restaurant. Emma fussed over Lucinda. Zach peered out the window. His head bobbed to the beat of music from his cellphone.

I checked behind often, curious about Lucinda's progress. For the first few blocks, she gagged at every turn.

"This is disgusting!" Zach moaned. He slid as close to the door as possible.

When we finally hit a straight stretch, the gagging eased. The cat purred. Zach relaxed.

Just before the highway, Mike turned down an unfamiliar street. Zach stiffened and frowned. "Where are we going? I thought you said we were in a hurry."

"A quick stop." Mike said. "Just a few minutes."

He turned a corner, then another and another. The car slowed as we drove under a wide stone arch. Leafy vines snaked up the pillars, partially covering a sign.

"This is your stop?" Zach said. "Really?"

Mike didn't say anything. He steered down a narrow gravel lane, past stone markers etched with letters and numbers. He turned several corners. Finally, he stopped.

Mike turned off the engine and opened the door. "Come. It won't take long."

I didn't need a second invitation. Neither did Emma. But Zach sullenly shook his head. "No way."

Lucinda gagged again, hurling a hairball coated with bits of food. Zach pulled out his earbuds and fled the car.

"Gawd. That's awful." He held his hand over his nose. "Is she going to do that the whole way?"

Mike smiled, but clearly his mind was on other things. He walked slowly past several stone slabs. He stopped at a dark grey one that was larger than the others. Atop the slab, an angel stood, wings outstretched, arms open wide. A single rose waved from a glass vase at the base of the stone. Tufts of grass bordered the rectangle of dirt spread before it.

I detected a familiar odour. I steered my nose through grass and weeds, around the slab to the rose. Of course. That mix of freshly cut grass and fragrant blossoms that Mike carried home on many of his afternoons away.

Mike straightened the rose and dusted the slab. He traced the letters on the stone with his finger. "Your mother didn't want to bring you to the cemetery after the funeral. It was winter, one of the coldest days on record…."

Emma grabbed Mike's hand. No one spoke for a long time.

Mike pulled a few weeds from the grass. "I come here most days. It's just something I like to do."

He put his hand on the stone angel and knelt on one knee. "Eva, I won't be able to visit for a few days," he whispered. "But I'll be thinking about you."

"Is that where Grandma is?" Emma asked, her voice soft and tiny.

"I'd like to think she's in a better place," Mike said.

He turned to a smaller stone standing beside Eva's. He traced his fingers across the words carved on it just as he had with hers. "I'll be thinking about you, too."

Zach leaned closer to read the words. Emma reached to touch the stone. "Who's that?"

"Did your mother ever tell you about Johnny?" Mike asked.

Emma shook her head. Zach shrugged.

Mike stood, one hand on the stone. His knee left a dent in the dirt. A small frown creased his forehead. "Johnny was your mother's twin. He died when she was two. I don't suppose she remembers much about him."

Zach moved closer. "How? I mean what happened?"

Mike shook his head. "The doctors couldn't find the cause. One day, he spiked a fever. The next day, he slipped into a coma and then…."

"He died," Emma whispered.

"Yes. He did."

Mike planted a kiss on Eva's stone. He ran a hand across Johnny's. Emma did the same, but Zach stood, hands in his pockets, as silent and still as the stone slabs.

On the way back to the car, I thought about Eva and Johnny. Were they together now? I promised myself that I would check the stars at night. I would look for two stars close together, a small one nestled beside a larger one. If Sirius had a place in heaven, why not Eva and Johnny?

Chapter 33

Sitting in the front beside Mike with the windows open, air streamed past me. It chased away the smell in the back seat. As the car veered around turns, Lucinda flattened her body against the kennel floor. Her eyes drooped. Her tail hung lifeless. She tried to curb the puke rising in her throat. Sometimes she succeeded. Sometimes not.

Gradually, the highway straightened. Slowly, Lucinda's nausea lessened. Finally, it vanished altogether. But the smell...the smell lingered.

Emma nodded off. Zach zoned out. Once in a while he muttered "disgusting", but mostly he gazed out the window, nodding to music pouring from his earbuds.

Mike relaxed, too. I watched him, fascinated by the expressions on his face. A small smile. A frown. Eyebrows lifting. Every small movement told a story. When I saw his eyes droop, I knew what that meant, too. He was falling asleep.

I pawed his arm. His head jerked up. "Sorry. Guess I'm more tired than I thought."

He turned on the radio. "This might help."

A song filled the front seat. Some guy wailed *Ain't got no loving feeling.*

Mike shook his head. "We can do better than that."

He punched buttons until he found a talk radio station. "Here. Let's try this."

Voices poured from the radio. A woman. A man. Another woman. Three people sharing information and sometimes arguing. Mostly they talked about how the country was being run, a topic Mike seemed to enjoy. "Darn right," he said more than once. "Absolutely."

As miles raced by, the people on the radio tackled other topics. Favourite eating places. Traffic. Technology. Among other things, I learned that The Kettle, a soup and sandwich shop, had just opened, the Skyway Bridge was clogged and should be avoided, and a hurricane was expected along Key West in Florida.

The landscape slowly changed. Barns replaced houses. Trees replaced bald prairie. The highway rose and fell as we climbed hills and dropped into valleys. Somehow Lucinda kept control of her stomach. She slept through much of the drive.

"Are we there yet?" Emma asked as we rolled past a huge sign.

Mike peered into the rear-view mirror. "No, Em. We have a long way to go, but we'll stop for a rest in the next town."

That was welcome news. After hours in the car, I was beginning to feel nauseous, too.

When a gas station appeared, Mike pulled up beside one of the pumps. "There's a little park over there." He pointed to a green space with picnic tables across the street. "We'll head there after."

As he filled up, Mike gazed at passing traffic. He

coughed a few times. I watched for signs of distress—hand over his chest, heavy wheezing—but there were none.

Suddenly, Mike tensed. A convertible pulled up to another pump. The door opened. A bearded man with a ponytail stepped out. He walked toward Mike, fists clenched at his side.

Emma who had been watching pointed. "Look, Zach. It's Dad."

Zach followed Emma's gaze. He grabbed Emma's arm. "Duck."

"Why?"

"Just do it."

Rick shouted something. Casually, Mike hung up the nozzle and climbed back into the car. He gunned the engine and roared out of the station, tires spinning. As we hit the highway, I glanced back. Rick was at the pump, shaking his fist, his mouth screaming words I couldn't hear.

As Mike careened down the road, I dug my claws into the seat, just barely keeping my balance. Behind, Lucinda whined.

Emma sobbed quietly. "I just wanted to see him."

"You know we can't," Zach said.

"I know."

Mike adjusted the mirror to see behind. "That was close." His voice was hoarse. "What are the chances that your father would pull into the same gas station at exactly the same time as us?"

"Yeah," Zach said. "Weird."

Emma wiped away a tear. Zach pulled out his cell-phone and handed it to his sister. "Here. Why don't you play a game?" He dug his notepad out of his backpack, flipped to a new page, and began drawing furiously.

"What are you drawing?" Mike asked.

"Nothing."

As the miles galloped by, Mike turned off the radio. Silence filled the car. Zach eventually nodded off. Emma played games. Lucinda hung on. I stared at the shifting landscape as the sun drifted west.

"I really have to pee." Emma said quietly.

Funny. So did I.

A few miles later, Mike pulled into a rest stop. Lucinda slept on, conked out by the meds Mike had given her. Zach and Emma hit the restroom. Mike opened the cooler and fished out a few sandwiches and a couple of drinks. Then he led me to a green area nearby. As I did my business, Mike peered up and down the highway.

"What the..." I heard him say before I could finish.

I looked to where he was staring. A convertible screamed past. The same convertible with the same bearded man at the wheel. Rick.

Mike tugged the leash. "Come on, kids," he yelled. "Hurry."

By the time Emma and Zach returned, Mike had the map spread across the steering wheel.

"What's wrong?" Zach asked.

"We're being followed." Mike traced his finger along the map. "I'm looking for a different route."

"Dad?" Emma peered down the highway. "Dad is following us?"

"Seems that way," Mike said.

He looked at the sky. Then he checked his watch. "It's getting late. I don't think I can drive much farther." He pointed to a dot on the map. "There's a town ahead about thirty minutes away. We'll look for a motel there."

As we pulled away, the convertible shot by again, heading the other way. Rick must have doubled back.

"What are you up to, Rick?" Mike said in a voice so soft I don't think anyone else heard it.

The next half hour felt like the longest ever. Mike fed me morsels of his peanut butter sandwich while Zach and Emma powered down theirs. Bleary-eyed Lucinda refused Emma's offers. She curled into a ball and slept.

I still had to pee. Every bump on the highway made it worse. Mostly, though, I was tired. I think we all were. Mike fidgeted in his seat, perhaps to keep awake but mostly because he kept checking the windows and mirrors for signs of Rick.

Our headlights cut through the growing darkness. By the time we stopped for the night at a small motel on the outskirts of the town, the moon was just beginning its rise across the sky. I was too tired to honour my promise to check the stars. If Eva and Johnny were there, it would have to wait.

That night, I slept beside Mike on his lumpy bed. Zach and Emma shared the other bed. I didn't hear them once, but I woke up often because of Lucinda. Free from the kennel, she roamed the room all night. As for Mike, he tossed and turned. Once I found him at the window, peering through a break in the curtains.

"This is not good," I heard him say. "Not good at all."

Chapter 34

It was still dark when Mike woke up Zach.

"It's only five," Zach moaned. "Why so early?"

Mike motioned Zach to the window. "I don't want to upset your sister," he whispered. "Look."

Zach pushed back the curtains. "Is that my dad's car?"

"Seems it is."

I snuck a peek, too. A convertible just like Rick's was parked a few doors down.

"He found us? How did he know we were here?"

Mike put his finger on his lips. "Shh. Not so loud." He glanced back at Emma, still asleep on the bed. "I've been wondering about that, too. It can't be just coincidence."

Mike woke Emma up soon after. She walked to the bathroom rubbing sleep from her eyes. "It's too early," she whined.

Mike clicked the leash to my collar and scooped up Lucinda. "Hurry kids. We'll be leaving in a few minutes."

Once outside, Mike led me to a patch of grass under the flickering neon sign. He put Lucinda down and removed my leash. "Okay, you two. Don't dawdle."

Lucinda tilted her head and blinked. She was a house cat. She did her business in a litter box, not outside. I don't think she knew what to do. I did, though.

While I peed, Mike studied the sky. "Looks like Sirius is rising," he said.

I followed his gaze to a sliver of pink along the horizon. I found Canis Major, then one star brighter than the others—Sirius—at the edge of the eastern sky. I looked for two other stars, one large, the other small, nestled together. Eva and Johnny. Were they there, too?

On the way back to our room, Mike stopped beside Rick's car to catch his breath. It was obvious even to me that Rick wasn't trying to hide. He'd parked under a streetlight as if he wanted us to notice.

"What are you up to?" Mike muttered.

Later, when Mike led Zach and Emma to the car, he warned them to be quiet. Zach gawked at Rick's convertible and shook his head. Emma didn't seem to notice.

Mike drove slowly out of the parking lot, lights out so as not to be seen. In a moment, we were barrelling along the highway, putting distance between Rick and us.

Ahead, snow-capped mountains reflected the rising sun. The highway stretched before us, a ribbon of grey pavement that seemed to go on forever. Trees edged the road. Except for the occasional oncoming car, the highway was empty.

Mike turned on the radio and lowered the volume so the sound didn't carry into the back seat. He sped down the highway, one hand on the steering wheel, the other on the console. He checked the mirrors often.

Emma slept. Zach played with his cellphone. Lucinda hung on to her breakfast. I dozed, grateful for the numbing hum of tires on the pavement.

How long I napped, I couldn't say. I woke up to the crunch of gravel and a blast of heat from the sun blazing through the windshield.

The car rolled to a stop.

"Where are we?" Emma stretched and yawned.

Zach peered out the window. "There's nothing here."

He was right. We were parked on the shoulder, close to a stand of pine trees. There wasn't a building or person in sight.

"Just listen," Mike cranked up the volume on the radio.

"Welcome back, folks," a man with a mellow voice said. "You're listening to Tech Talk on station CXWT. For those just joining us, we've been chatting with Elaine Scorer, a cellphone consultant at Speedy-Talk Industries. So, Elaine, before the commercial break we were discussing cellphone security."

"Yes, Roger," a soft voice replied. "Many people don't realize how much information their cellphone holds or how that information is sometimes shared without the user's knowledge."

Zach leaned forward. "Why are we listening to this? I thought we were in a hurry."

Mike put his finger to his lips. "Just pay attention." He turned up the volume another notch.

"Right, Elaine," Roger said. "You were telling us

how hackers can tap into a phone's settings to pinpoint a person's location. Can you elaborate?"

"Well, it's really not all that difficult. You don't even have to be texting or making a call for someone to breach security and determine your precise location. You just have to be near transmission towers and have some knowledge......"

Mike lowered the volume. "Zach," he said, turning around. "Remember what we talked about before? How you father seems to be know exactly where we are?"

"Yeah. So?"

Mike held up his cellphone. "So, I think it might be through our phones."

"But I was only listening to music and playing games."

"According to this expert, it doesn't matter."

Mike ran his hand over his chin. "When did you get the phone?"

"Last year." Zach peered through the gap between the front seats. "It was a gift. Sort of..."

"Sort of?"

"I never thought..." Zach's stared at the cellphone like he was seeing it for the first time. "My dad bought it for me just before he moved out."

He shifted uneasily. "I thought it was his way of trying to make up for the trouble he caused, but...." He looked up. "Maybe not."

Emma fidgeted. "Why are we here?"

"We'll be on the road again in just a minute," Mike said.

I peered over the seat. I expected an explosion of anger from Zach, but he just studied his cellphone, not uttering a word.

Finally, Zach looked up. "We have to disable our phones. If we pull out the batteries, that might do it. I'm not really sure."

"Let's do it then."

Zach nodded. "I guess, but..."

A small smile broke out on his lips. "I have an idea. Are you willing to sacrifice your phone?"

Chapter 35

Zach unbuckled his seat belt, grabbed the map, and opened the door. He spread the map on the hood of the car and called Mike to join him. They huddled over the map, heads together. I studied their faces, their hands, the movements of their bodies. What was their plan?

Zach jabbed the map. Mike traced his finger across it. They peered up and down the highway. Zach smiled. So did Mike. They nodded and laughed. Then Mike slapped Zach on the back. Zach high-fived Mike in return.

"Coop," Mike said as he slid back into the car. "You'll have to trade places with Zach."

It only made sense. Zach was the navigator now, the guardian of the map. While Mike tore down the highway, Zach gave directions.

"Ten miles more," he said as Mike passed a slower car.

Sitting in the back seat, squished against the window without the benefit of a stiff breeze to chase away the smell of puke, I hung on as Mike charged down the highway. Lucinda meowed and scratched the walls of the kennel. Luckily, she settled once the road straightened.

Zach consulted the map and studied the road. "We just passed mile marker 25. It's a mile further. It will be on your right."

A minute later, Mike slowed and turned into a roadside rest stop. A half-dozen cars and trucks filled the small parking lot. Semi-trailers lined the curb, some with engines still running.

"Okay, everyone out," Mike said.

Emma raced to the restroom. I followed Mike as he carried Lucinda to the pet area. Lucinda looked at the field of grass, bewildered and confused. Finally, she chose a patch, meowing as she did her business. I did mine, too, dousing fence posts and blades of grass to claim them as my own.

Zach wandered across the parking lot. He held his cellphone in his hand. When he neared a half-ton truck, he side-checked to see if anyone was looking. He dropped the phone onto the truck bed. Then he walked back with his hands in his pockets, a wide smile on his face.

Zach nodded to Mike and gave him the thumbs up. Mike nodded back.

Back in the car, Mike wheeled onto the highway again. As we drove, he hummed a tune and tapped the steering wheel.

"Up ahead, fifteen miles," Zach announced. "Look for Route 85."

Wedged between Lucinda and the door, I studied the landscape. Evergreens streamed past the window. Boulders lined the highway, some alone, some clustered together, some perched on top of others.

We slowed when we drove through a small town and passed a gas station. Mike glanced at the fuel gauge and checked the mirrors. "We should be good for a while. I'd rather not stop. Not here anyways."

A few miles farther, Zach pointed to a sign. "There. Route 85."

Mike punched the gas pedal. As we shot past the turnoff to Route 85, Emma leaned forward. "Weren't you supposed to turn there?"

Zach looked at his sister. "We will. Just not yet."

Miles further, Mike pulled off the highway. He steered around potholes and ruts along a dusty road. Lucinda coughed, gagged, and heaved. Fortunately for all of us, she had nothing left to give.

We drove past freshly tilled fields, then turned down a narrow road. We bounced and churned dust as Mike drove. He slowed as we crossed a wooden bridge. On the other side, he stopped and pointed to a rickety barn in a neighbouring field.

Mike handed his cellphone to Zach. "Will you do the honours?"

"Gladly."

Zach strode across the field with Mike's cellphone in his hand. He disappeared in the barn. When he resurfaced a moment later, the cellphone was gone.

"Deed done," he said, climbing back into the car.

He grinned at Mike. Mike smiled back.

"That should do it," Mike said.

We returned the way we had come, down the dusty road to the highway, down the highway to the turnoff for Route 85.

As Mike wheeled onto Route 85, Zach looked behind. "All clear."

Only then did I realize the brilliance of Zach's

plan. We were taking a different route to Madison. By now Zach's phone was probably somewhere else, going wherever the truck was heading. Mike's phone was tucked inside a barn along a deserted road, far from the turnoff. If Rick was tracking either one of them, he would end up somewhere else.

Chapter 36

Route 85 snaked through woods, climbed hills, and plunged into valleys. Unlike the highway with its smooth pavement and wide lanes, Route 85 was a rugged trail. Mike slowed around curves and swerved to dodge rough patches in the heaving asphalt.

"This used to be the main road to Madison." Mike clenched his teeth and tightened his grip on the steering wheel. "When they built the new highway, they left this one, but it hasn't been serviced in years."

We rode for an hour, jostling over bumps and veering around hairpin curves. Except for one truck loaded with logs, the road was deserted.

Numbed by the dullness of the terrain, we settled into silence. My mind drifted. Buck. Max. Sparky. They appeared in my head, looking like ghostly figures from a distant past. It seemed a lifetime ago that I had been at Derby. I had a new owner now, a new home, a new family. I'd even warmed up to Lucinda. I think she'd warmed up to me, too.

Zach was a wild card, though. He was unpredictable and moody. Even so, I felt a strange kinship with him. He'd been rejected, too. We both bore scars from our troubled pasts. Not just the physical kinds. We shared the invisible ones, the scars that are etched on souls. Those take more time to heal.

Emma's voice broke through my thoughts. "Grandpa, can I take Lucy out of the kennel?"

"Sure," Mike adjusted the rear-view mirror. "But you'll have to hang on to her."

Lucinda meowed softly as Emma pried her out. She looked ghastly—eyes wide, fur matted, ears flat against her skull.

"Poor Lucy. You've been in there forever," Emma said.

I looked out the window again. The terrain had changed. Instead of sparse clumps of trees, thick, towering clusters lined both sides of the narrow road. With trees so large and tight, it seemed more like night now than day.

The road twisted. Mike cranked the wheel and pumped the brakes often. We rumbled along, pitched against the doors at every turn. I glanced at Lucinda. She looked back at me with glassy eyes.

Suddenly, Mike braked and pulled over beside a giant pine. He looked left, then right, then down at the map. "Which way?"

Zach peered out the window. "I don't know."

Ahead, the road forked. There were no signs to mark left or right. Both options looked the same.

Mike spread the map across the steering wheel. He angled it to catch the fading light. "There's nothing marked on the map."

He rubbed his chin and peered over the hood. "If I had to guess, I'd say we should go right. What do you think?"

Zach nodded. "Okay."

Later, as we tore down our chosen route, as the road thinned even more, as the car lurched ever deeper into the forest, I wondered if this was the right decision. Judging from Mike, Zach, and Emma's pale faces, I think they wondered, too.

And Lucinda? She dove to the floor and hid below Emma's legs.

Chapter 37

The road tunnelled through the forest, more narrow and rough with each curve. Branches on both sides joined overhead. They blocked out what little sun was left. Mike switched on the headlights as we bounced along the rutted trail.

A stream raced beside us. It ran so fast that it seemed to keep pace with the car. I watched as logs floated by and smashed against rocks that jutted out of the shallow water, shooting chunks of bark in the spray.

Mike manned the steering wheel, his knuckles white as the car pitched down the road. "Like riding a bucking bronco," he said.

I stuck my head through the gap between the front seats and balanced unsteadily on the console. Zach spread the map across his knees. He hung on to it with one hand while he clutched the door handle with the other. He glanced at Mike. Then he looked at the dashboard.

"We're pretty low on gas. Are we going to make it?"

"Let's hope so."

Zach studied the map. His finger traced a jagged line that ended at a small dot. "There isn't a town for miles. And we're still a long way from Madison."

Mike glanced down. "Where exactly are we?"

"Here, I think." Zach pointed to the map.

Mike leaned over for a closer look, "Hmm…Maybe."

So much can happen in just a few seconds. In this case, with Mike's eyes on the map, he missed a turn in the road. Two wheels slid off the broken asphalt. The car veered sharply and grazed a tree.

"Holy…" Mike cranked the steering wheel to bring the car back on the road. But the slope was too steep and the bank was too slick. The car skidded sideways.

Mike slammed on the brakes. "God, no," he muttered.

Emma screamed. Zach flung the map aside and grabbed the dashboard. Lucinda slid to the floor again. I clawed the seat.

"God, no!" Mike yelled again.

He glanced back. I saw panic in his eyes. "Hang on everyone! Brace yourself!"

The car careened over rocks and tore at branches alongside the stream.

"We're gonna crash," Zach yelled.

From somewhere below Emma's feet, Lucinda screeched. I dug in my heels and braced for impact.

I must have closed my eyes at that point. I have little memory of the fall. It happened so fast. One second, we were on land. The next, we were airborne, sailing off a rocky ledge into the stream.

The car clipped a jutting rock and careened off another, then landed with a thunderous splash. My head smacked the window. Emma's head hit the seat in front of her. Lucinda clawed the floor mat, not uttering so much as a screech.

The airbags deployed with a bang, pinning Mike and Zach to their seats. Just as quickly, they deflated with a whoosh.

The front bumper of the car crumpled, crunched by the impact. The car dipped. The tail end rose, then slowly fell. We drifted a few feet, scraping over rocks, then finally the car lurched to a stop.

No one spoke or moved.

"Is everyone okay?" Mike finally asked. Blood trickled down his forehead. He wiped it away with a trembling hand.

Zach looked back. "I think so."

Emma nodded. She pulled herself upright, hands quivering. Already a small bruise coloured her forehead.

"Coop, how about you?" Mike glanced over his shoulder.

I barked, but it was a feeble response. My head ached. So did my teeth. I must have been clenching my jaw.

"Lucy?" Mike reached around for the cat.

Poor Lucinda. She looked wretched. Even I felt sorry for her.

Suddenly, the car shifted.

"Oh no." Zach's head jerked up. He peered out the window. "I think we're moving!"

Chapter 38

I peered out the window, too. Trees along the bank seemed to be moving, only I knew they weren't really. We were the ones moving, pushed by the swift current.

Mike clutched the steering wheel as the tires bumped along the stream bed. Zach and Emma grabbed the door handles. Lucinda leaped onto the seat and flung herself at the closed window in a foolish attempt to escape. When that failed, she cowered under Emma's feet. I pressed my nose against the glass. I yipped. I didn't mean to. It just slipped out.

Carried by the water, the car drifted, grinding over rocks and twisting with the current.

"Crap…"…" Zach muttered. He added a few more words, but I don't think I should repeat them.

"I'm scared," Emma whispered.

Mike reached behind to tap her knee. He flashed a weak smile. "We'll be all right. You'll see."

Zach looked at Mike. Mike looked at Zach. Both of their faces were chalky white. Emma gathered wild-eyed Lucinda in her arms. "You're scared too, aren't you Lucy?"

I yipped. *What about me? I'm scared, too.*

We were at the mercy of the current. The car bumped and scraped downstream. Suddenly, it jerked to a stop.

Zach looked outside. "We're not moving anymore."

Mike peered over the hood. "We must be hung up on a rock."

We all looked. Even Lucinda. She squeezed past me to plaster her face against my window.

Zach tapped Mike on the shoulder. He pointed to the floor. "Water. We're taking on water."

I glanced down. Water trickled through the rusted edge of the door, pooling into a puddle on the mat.

"Keep calm, everyone." Mike looked behind. "The stream is really shallow here. We'll be okay."

But we weren't okay. I knew that from the way Mike's voice trembled, from the whiteness of his knuckles and the hunch of his shoulders.

I tried to keep calm for Emma's sake, but she probably knew I wasn't. My tail drooped. My legs trembled. I looked at Mike, then at Emma, and then at the stream with its fast-moving riffles. Debris swept past the car—twigs, branches, a log. They crashed against rocks that jutted out of the water, then they disappeared in a spray of mist ahead.

Mike rolled down his window. A roar filled the car. "Rapids," he whispered.

His voice was so low, I don't think anyone else heard him.

"What?" Zach asked.

Just then the car shifted.

"What's happening?" Emma leaned forward to peer over the seat.

An uneasy quiet settled over us. The car shuddered.

Grating sounds radiated through the floor as rocks scraped the underside.

Mike put his hand on Zach's shoulder, "No one move." He said something else, but his voice was lost to the roar of the rapids.

Zach shrugged off Mike's hand and opened the door. Water spilled inside and seeped across the floor.

"What are you doing?" Mike reached to stop him, but Zach was already on the edge of his seat with his feet dangling above the rushing water.

"I think I can make it."

Before Mike could say anything more, Zach slipped his backpack over his shoulder and leaned back to grab the map. He stepped out and placed one foot on the rock closest to the car.

"Be careful!" Mike shouted.

I craned my neck for a better view. I saw now what Zach had noticed. A series of rocks jutted out of the water. They led from the car to the far-off bank.

Zach stretched out his arms to maintain his balance. He edged forward, one slick rock at a time.

"That's the way to do it," Mike shouted.

Emma slid over. She pressed her face against the glass. Even Lucinda crept closer, so close I could smell the vomit on her breath.

A branch swept by, followed by other floating objects—an empty glass jar, still sealed; a fence post, weathered and bleached. From the corner of my eye, I caught a glimpse of a log approaching.

I barked. *Zach, look out.*

I don't think Zach heard me. He was bent over, one foot on a rock, the other searching for a grip on the rock ahead. He didn't see it coming.

The log bounced against the rock and clipped Zach's ankle. He teetered for a moment and fought to regain his balance, then finally found his footing again. When he shifted his backpack and glanced behind, I saw pain on his face.

Emma's face turned white. "Zach's hurt," she whispered.

Mike slid over to Zach's side of the car. "Hold on. I'm coming."

"No, stay there!" Zach shouted.

He shifted the backpack and scanned the stream for other drifting objects. Then he hobbled across the remaining rocks.

Emma clapped her hands. "I knew you could do it, Zach!"

Once on the bank, Zach waved. Then he sat down. He winced when he pulled the shoe off his injured leg. He winced again when he peeled off the sock.

"Our turn," Mike said to Emma. "Don't worry. We'll be okay, I promise."

"I'm scared."

"Me, too. But we'll be careful."

Mike hung on to the door as he planted a foot on the same rock Zach had used. He reached for Emma's hand. "Come. One step at a time."

Mike looked at Lucinda, scrunched below the seat. Then he looked at me, clawing the window. "Just stay here. Stay still. I'll be back for you."

But the way he said it, his voice shaking, his breathing shallow and wheezy, I doubted he would make it. Mike was unsteady on firm ground and this was even more risky.

Mike held Emma's hand and coaxed her along. "There. There. That's the way to do it."

Mike led Emma from one rock to the next. Part way across, Mike's foot slipped. He released Emma's hand, teetered, and struggled to keep his balance. So did Emma, who straddled the rocks behind Mike. She reached ahead to grab Mike's hand.

I watched the whole thing from the car. I felt useless. I couldn't help them except to bark encouragement, which I did, loudly and often. *Be careful. You can do it.*

Finally, Mike found his footing again. He reached for Emma. Together, they inched across the last few rocks.

On the bank, Mike and Zach shared a few words. Zach pointed to the car. He stepped towards the stream. Mike shook his head. He grabbed Zach's arm. Zach pried off Mike's hand and pointed to the ground. He said something. Not that I could hear, but I'm good at interpreting gestures and facial expressions. I'm pretty sure Zach said, "Stay here, I've got this."

While Mike rested under a tree, Zach made two trips across the swift stream. First, he flung Lucinda over one shoulder and forged across the rocks, one unsteady step at a time. Lucinda hung on, draped like a wet rag over Zach's shoulder, her yellow eyes wide as saucers.

I watched, nervous for them, but nervous for me, too. I was alone now, the only one left in the car. My chances depended on their success. I barked and pawed the window to cheer them on.

When Zach came for me, he wrapped me in my blanket. He heaved me over his shoulder and clung to the car door until he found his footing.

"Hang on, Coop."

I dug my heels into Zach's t-shirt. With each of his steps, I glanced upstream, worried that another log might topple us. I was prepared to bark a warning if I spotted one, but only a few small branches careened against the rocks, none large enough to do damage.

Midway across, Zach stopped and shifted me to his other shoulder. I caught a glimpse of his pale face, the furrows on his brow, his clenched teeth.

Zach patted my back. "We're almost there, Coop."

When we reached the shore, Mike greeted us with an outstretched arm. Zach grabbed hold and hobbled a few steps before putting me down. His face was wet from the spray. His hands shook.

"Just one more trip," Zach turned back to the stream. "We'll need a few things from the car."

Mike grabbed Zach's arm. "Stay here. I'll go."

But neither one went. At that moment, the car shivered. The tires slid on the slick ledge and we watched as a log struck the car, knocking it off its perch. The car floated, twisting and turning until it reached the rapids. Then the hood dipped, the trunk rose, and the whole thing disappeared into the foamy spray.

Chapter 39

People react to disaster in different ways. Mike collapsed on the ground, not saying a word. Emma gazed at the spot where the car had disappeared as if she could wish its return. She didn't even notice Lucinda, who curled around her legs demanding attention.

Zach slumped to the ground. He nursed his injured leg and rocked from side to side. "Now what? Now what?"

I lay beside Mike and rested my head on his chest. Over the thunder of the stream, I heard his heart pounding, skipping beats like a shoddy drummer. He drew deep breaths, gasping with each one.

"Now what?" he asked, echoing Zach.

And that's the way it was for a long while. The five of us, lost not just in thoughts, but lost also in a more real way.

The stream cut a swath through the thick forest. On one side, too far and dangerous for us to reach, was the twisted, deserted road that might have led us to Madison. On our side, wilderness with no clear path to guide the way out.

"We've lost everything," Zach said, breaking the silence.

"Well, not quite." Mike smiled weakly. "Coop has his blanket."

Mike's remark broke the spell. Zach chuckled. Emma spun around and finally noticed Lucinda pawing at her feet.

"Oh Lucy, what a mess you are!" She picked up the soggy cat and cradled her in her arms. "I'm so glad you're okay."

Mike tried getting up but immediately sat down again. "I just need another minute."

"What are we going to do?" Zach asked again.

While Mike rested, Emma cuddled Lucinda. Zach swabbed his leg. I moved in for a closer look. Not that I have medical training, but even I could tell by his swollen and bloody ankle that he was in trouble. To his credit, Zach didn't complain. He covered his leg and kept the bad news to himself. I suspect he didn't want to worry the others.

Zach spread the damp map on the ground in front of Mike. "Where do you suppose we are?"

Mike leaned forward. "Well, I'm only guessing, but I think we're here." He tapped his finger on the map.

I crawled nearer to see for myself. Mike's spot seemed just like any other spot on the map.

"See." Mike moved his finger across the map. "There's the road. Here's the stream. See how the stream widens. That's where I think we are."

Zach squinted at the fine print. "Midland Rapids," he read.

To me, everything on the map looked the same.

"There's Madison," Mike said. "And we're here."

Zach shook his head. "That's a long way. And there's not much in between. Hills and forest. A ridge."

"But look." Mike tapped the map again. "There's a rail line near the ridge."

"So?"

"The rail line leads straight to Madison. We just have to find it, then follow it."

Zach bit his cheek, ran his hand through his hair, and gazed at the darkening sky. He didn't say it in words, but I knew what he was thinking. We'd lost everything to the stream, not only backpacks, suitcases, and the cooler, but Mike's pills, too.

They slept. Not me. Just the others.

Zach rolled the clothes he pulled out of his backpack to use as pillows for Mike and Emma. They curled into a heap for warmth near a fallen log, Emma hugging Lucinda. Lulled by a soft breeze and the roar of water, they drifted into an exhausted sleep.

But I couldn't. I snuggled beside Mike. My thin blanket provided little warmth for us. Each time I closed my eyes, something jarred me awake. Mike's ragged breath drawing in and out. The irregular beat of his heart, hammering in his chest. Moans from Zach. Soft sighs from Emma.

I heard sounds in the forest and they chased sleep away, too. Owls hooting. Leaves rustling. Far away, wolves howling.

And the stars. They also kept me awake. The sky was so free of clouds and city lights that they shone brighter than I'd ever seen before. I remembered my promise. Eva and Johnny. Where were they?

I gazed skyward and searched through the maze.

I looked for two stars nestled together, one large, the other small. But there were so many. I couldn't find them and gave up trying.

I crawled out of the heap and sat beside the stream. At night, it seemed less a threat than before. I couldn't see the distant bank. I couldn't see the rapids that had swallowed the car.

What would become of us? We had no food. We had few supplies, just the things in Zach's backpack. By now, Jess would know something was wrong since we hadn't arrived as scheduled. But even if she alerted the police, they wouldn't know where to find us. We were far off our planned route, without cellphones or other ways to reach her.

I thought of the map. Madison, a dot near the top. Our position miles away. The thick forest, hills, and a ridge in between. The slender rail line that offered hope if only we could reach it.

How could we? Mike was frail and without the pills he needed. Zach's ankle? He would have to hop and hobble over difficult terrain. Emma. Lucinda. I didn't think either had the strength or endurance to make it.

And me? A wiener dog, old, arthritic, with hip problems. Hopeless.

Hours crept by. Mike snorted and wheezed. Zach rolled over, groaned softly, then fell asleep again. Emma and Lucinda didn't move, not once.

Slowly, darkness faded. Along the east, the sky took on a different hue—the pinks and golds of a new day. As the sun broke above the horizon, I watched the stars fade.

One cluster caught my attention. Canis Major.

I sat up. One star shone brighter than the others. The Dog Star. Sirius who had earned a place in heaven.

Others might scoff. Ridiculous. Heaven—if there is a heaven at all—is not up there. And people don't turn into stars when they die. And if people don't, then dogs—even the best kinds—certainly don't either. How silly.

That morning, though, I believed they did.

Chapter 40

Already the heat was building. There wasn't a cloud in sight. The day promised to be another scorcher.

I searched the sky again. If Sirius had a star, wouldn't others as loyal, brave, and trustworthy have stars, too? Like Bobbie, the Wonder Dog. All that time alone, day and night, trotting up mountains and through deserts so he could be with his owner. Wouldn't that qualify him for a place above? Hachiko, too—loyal for so long to his owner. Salty—so faithful to Omar. Shouldn't they have stars, too?

I checked the sleeping heap. Zach had his arm around his sister. Lucinda was comfortably squished between Emma and Mike. Mike lay on his back, his hand on his chest, his breath rumbling in and out.

No one told Bobbie the Wonder Dog what to do or where to go. No one ordered Salty to help Omar when terrorists struck the World Trade Center. Same with Hachiko. He kept coming to the train station on his own. Was it instinct? Were they just smarter than other dogs? Or did they summon a higher power?

I didn't know. Then again, humans didn't either. Not even with all their clever testing. Take Laika. All those wires running to machines as she rocketed into space. What did that tell scientists about her? Not a lot. Her pulse, her breathing, but nothing about her thoughts or feelings. Nothing about the emotions that swirled through her body. Nothing about her soul.

For all their smarts, humans don't really know what goes on inside dogs' heads. They don't know what makes dogs do what they do. Perhaps they never will. Maybe that's one of the greatest mysteries of all time.

I saw the map clutched in Zach's hand. I pictured it again. The stream curled through the forest, travelling east. The rail line ran north-south. At one point, it bridged the stream.

Follow the stream. Reach the rail line. Head straight to Madison, to Jess. Simple.

I had gone only a few steps when Zach sat up and yawned. He looked at Emma, still asleep, clutching Lucinda. He looked at Mike, curled under my blanket. Then he saw me.

"Coop?"

I turned, took a few steps away, then hesitated when Zach called again.

"Coop, wait."

Mike mumbled something. Emma drew Lucinda closer. Neither woke up as Zach hobbled over, cringing with each step.

"Are you leaving us, Coop?"

How could I tell him?

But I didn't have to. Zach looked back at Mike. He saw the blanket. He knew I would come back for it, for them.

"You are the only one who can do it," he said.

Zach crouched beside me. He ran his hand along

my back. His fingers lingered over my collar. "Wait a minute, Coop."

He fetched his backpack, dug through it, and pulled out his earbuds.

"This might help," he said as he tied them to my collar.

Then he took out his notepad, tore out a sheet, and scratched a hurried note. He tied it to the earbuds. "Go, Coop. We're counting on you."

I went a short distance, then stopped to look back. Zach was still standing where I'd left him. He nodded and then waved.

I ran. I followed the twisting stream past the rapids where the car had disappeared. Soon the forest closed around me and, within minutes, I stopped to question my judgement. What was I thinking? I was no Bobbie or Hachiko. I was Coop, a tired old dachshund. Words I'd heard all my life rattled through my head. "Look! A wiener dog! A sausage meister! A teenie weenie! Ha, ha!"

I looked at the sky. The pinks and golds had disappeared, replaced by a brilliant blue. Sirius was no longer visible, but I knew he was still there, hanging on to his place in heaven. He wouldn't quit, would he?

I shook off my doubt and ran. The stream snaked through the forest, past clutches of tightly packed pines and aspens. It coursed through meadows too, grassy patches that seemed like islands adrift in a sea of trees. Before long, the muddy bank gave way to rocks and pebbles. The stream widened. The flat terrain evolved into hills and bluffs.

I wasn't built for speed. I wasn't built for steep climbs either. Not with my arthritis and short legs. And I certainly wasn't built for brush and tall grass. Burrs snagged my belly. They stuck like glue, and the farther I ran, the larger the collection grew. They rubbed against my legs. They stuck to my ears. I stopped to pull them off, but they resisted. I swear they dug their barbs even deeper.

The sun blazed, the rocks boiled, and my pads took a beating. When I tired, I rested. When thirst sapped my strength, I drank from the stream. And when hunger struck ... well there was nothing to eat. I tried chewing bark and even the pesky burrs, but they only made me heave. I thought of Lucinda, gagging at each turn. So this was what it was like.

For long stretches, I had the forest and stream all to myself. Other than a few screaming crows and bounding rabbits, no other life forms seemed to exist. I was lulled into believing that I was alone.

I wasn't.

Around one turn, I felt eyes boring into my backside. A chill crept up my spine. I glanced at a cluster of aspens. The air was still—not even a wisp of a breeze—and yet the leaves trembled. I caught a glimpse of movement, a shifting shadow. Was it a cougar? Maybe a bear? Slow and small, I would be a tasty morsel for a hungry predator.

I sped ahead, but the encounter spooked me. I checked over my shoulder often and scanned the trees on either side, wary of hidden danger. With every step, my anxiety climbed as my imagination took over. I was the hunted here. I was in territory that was not my own.

By mid-afternoon, I was so sore and tired that I couldn't take another step. I found a shady and secluded nook. I lay down on my side, careful not to put pressure on the burrs. Immediately, I fell asleep.

I must have slept for hours, unaware that the sun had shifted and the day was ending. When I finally awoke, the forest was shrouded in shadows. I'd never felt so alone. I'd spent my life indoors in the company of others. Even my most neglectful owners had given me a bed. Even Ruth at Derby had come to say goodnight.

I trekked on, lonelier than I'd ever felt before.

Chapter 41

The moon slowly rose to guide me. I plodded on, swallowing my fear and raging hunger. When I couldn't see ahead, I trusted my ears and nose. I followed the sound of rushing water. I tracked the sweet scent of pine and the earthy smell of decaying leaves carried on the soft breeze.

When I grew scared, I thought of Bobbie. He must have been scared, too. All that time alone, day and night, summer and winter. I thought of Hachiko, Salty, Balto, and all the others who had achieved greatness. No one gave up when the going got tough.

Mike, I thought of him often. Zach and Emma, too. They must be just as hungry and cold. I pictured them huddled in the clearing. Was I their only hope?

And Jess, what was she doing? I imagined her sitting by the window of her new home, gazing at the blackness outside, wondering where we were and praying that we were all right.

Eventually, the shoreline narrowed. It was replaced by a steep wall of rock. Forced to steer around it, I entered the dark forest.

By moonlight, shadows played across the ground. Trees took on odd shapes. An owl hooted. A chorus of other sounds followed—frogs croaking, crickets chirping. Far away, wolves howled. I shivered and kept going.

Gradually, the forest thinned. I entered a clearing ringed by tall trees. I no longer heard the rush of the stream and that worried me. Was I lost? Then, as I reached the middle of the clearing, I heard new sounds. The screech of wheels. The thunder of a train. I moved faster, certain that the rail line was near.

Eventually, the sound of the train faded. The forest grew quiet. Too quiet. I listened, scarcely breathing. Had I veered off the trail?

A twig snapped. A light wavered between the trees, growing closer. I heard voices. Then the clink of metal.

"You sure this is the spot? It's miles from nowhere," a man said.

I shivered. The voice sounded like Rick's.

"Yeah, this is it. I know this place like the back of my hand," said another man.

Leaves rustled. Branches parted. A creature dragging a clanking chain stepped out of the shadows. I hid behind a tree and gulped down the panic crawling up my throat.

Two men followed. One held a flashlight. He was tall, lean, and dressed in a blend of brown and greens. A rifle hung over one shoulder. The other man, dressed in the same colours, was shorter with a round belly that hung over his belt. Instead of a rifle, he carried a large crossbow.

I breathed easier. Neither of the men was Rick. But still, I recognized the men's outfits. One of my previous owners used to dress this way. Whenever he donned clothes like this, he'd be gone for hours. When he returned, a rifle in one hand, he smelled of death.

Often he brought back a trophy—a limp duck or a glassy-eyed rabbit dripping blood.

"Butch, wait up." The tall man grabbed the chain to reel the creature in.

"That dog of yours is useless," the short one said. "Why'd ya bring him anyways, Ted?

Ted pulled the dog closer and ruffled his fur. "Never you mind him, Butch. You're a good doggie, aren't you?"

Butch was the size of a small horse. His sad eyes drooped. Skin hung in loose folds from his jaw. Drool dripped from his mouth like sticky icicles. Butch looked a little like Spike from Derby, a bloodhound with a quick temper.

Butch stood on his hind legs and draped himself over Ted's shoulders. He slathered Ted's face with his long tongue and coated his head with gooey slobber.

"That's a good boy," Ted said again as he scratched Butch's back. "Now, find a spot to do your business."

Butch sniffed a tree, raised his leg, and gave it a good soaking. Later, Ted reeled in the chain and tied it to a stump. "You'll see, Sam. Tomorrow, Butch is going to come in handy. He's got a killer instinct. We make a great team."

Sam lit a lantern and set it on a stump. While the men pitched a small tent and rolled out sleeping bags, Butch sat on his haunches and gazed with dull eyes at the forest.

"Make yourself useful, Ted," said Sam. "Round up some firewood while I get dinner started."

Ted propped his rifle against a rock. Taking long

steps, he strode across the clearing, aiming his flashlight right and left. Now and then, he bent down to pick up twigs and branches. He threw them into a pile as he muttered under his breath, "Sure, make me do the heavy lifting."

"What's that you say?" Sam asked.

"Nothing."

Ted grumbled some more as he passed my hiding place. My heart hammered in my chest. Then my stomach growled. Loudly.

Butch barked fiercely and lurched, yanking the chain.

Ted waved the flashlight across the clearing. "You hear that, Sam?"

Sam reached for his bow. He passed the rifle to Ted. "Hear what?"

Ted shouldered the rifle. "Not sure. It came from over there."

A beam of light splayed across the tree. I ducked. The light danced to another tree, then back to mine, then on to another. Scarcely breathing, I stole a peek.

Butch howled. He pawed the ground and lurched again.

"Easy Butch," Ted said. "It's probably nothing."

Butch sniffed the air. His ears twitched. He locked his gaze on my hiding place. Then he sat on his haunches and bayed.

"Shut that dog up, will ya?" Sam yelled. "We're not supposed to be here, remember."

"I told you before, nobody ever comes here."

"Well, I'd rather be careful. Fines are steep for out-of-season hunting. The last thing I need is a criminal record."

"Yeah. Yeah. You worry too much. Tomorrow, when you bag your first kill, you'll see things differently."

Butch howled again. He seemed as eager to kill as the two men.

Ted waved the flashlight around. "Calm down, Butch. It's nothing."

Butch stretched his long body across the ground, his head almost in the can of beans that Sam was opening. The smell of food drifted to me, teasing my empty stomach. What I wouldn't have given for just a taste.

Ted dumped an armful of firewood on the ground. He broke branches into small pieces, stacked them in criss-crossed layers, and crinkled up a sheet of paper to stick inside.

"You're not lighting that now, are you?" Sam said. "It will be seen for miles."

"Course not. I'm not stupid. Just getting ready for morning. Nothing like a hot breakfast to start the day."

I couldn't move. I was only a small mouthful for Butch, and Ted looked nervous and eager to use his rifle. I was a likely target—old, slow, and the colour of just about every other animal in the forest.

I spent the next few hours with one eye on the men, another on Butch, waiting for an opportunity to make my move.

Chapter 42

The two men took forever to fall asleep. They sat on stumps around the stack of firewood, ate cold beans, and drank a few beers. Ted let Butch lick the can clean.

The men's voices carried across the clearing. They talked about the morning's hunt, the tactics they would use, and how they would butcher their kill.

Now and then, Butch growled and Ted would wave the flashlight. "Did you hear that?"

Each time, Sam calmed him down. "Nah. It's nothing. Come on, drink up."

In the forest, away from city lights, the stars shone brightly. I looked for Bobbie, Salty, Hachiko, and the others. I looked for Eva and Johnny, too. But there were so many stars, I couldn't tell one from the other. Then, for some reason, I thought of Lucinda. Did cats have places in heaven, too?

"Guess we better get some shut-eye," one man said, interrupting my thoughts.

The two slipped into the tent and talked some more. When Butch whined, Ted dragged him into the tent. Sam complained, but eventually gave in. The chain rattled. Butch woofed once, then the forest grew quiet.

I waited. Then I waited some more.

I knew now that the rail line was close. That meant Madison was, too. All I had to do was flee the clearing, forge through the trees, and climb the ridge. I was sure the stream was nearby. The bridge leading to the rail line, too.

A wolf howled. Others joined in. A chorus of yips and bays filled the air. The wolves sounded closer than before.

No sound came from the tent. Maybe Ted had given Butch the same medication that Mike used with Lucinda. The dog didn't whimper, not even when the wolves hit their loudest notes.

While the wolves were still howling, I crept across the crisp grass. Near the tent, I stopped. All three were snoring, each taking a turn.

I crept on, then doubled back. I found the tree that Butch had soaked. I lifted my leg and branded it as my own. *Take that, Butch. This one's mine.*

At the edge of the clearing, I picked up the pace. I wound through tall trees and past a rocky outcropping. The collection of burrs on my belly had grown. With each step, the prickly tips chafed my underside, rubbing the skin raw. I huffed and panted, and pushed past the pain in my joints and torn pads as I climbed up the steep slope to the top of the ridge.

A wall of rock rose behind the bald ridge, but the view in the other direction was spectacular. With the moon and stars hanging overhead, I saw traces of my journey. The thick forest sprawling for miles. The stream curling through it like a snake. The clearing where the two men and Butch slept.

I rested on the ridge, exhausted, and looked

towards the horizon. Somewhere in the far-off darkness, Mike, Emma, and Zach waited. And Lucinda, of course. Were they asleep?

When I looked to the right, I saw a thin shadow that led to lights in the distance. The rail line. The lights of Madison. Jess was there, waiting and worrying.

Chapter 43

I awoke hours later, jarred out of a deep sleep by a feeling that something was wrong. In the east, the sun had just started to rise above the horizon. I found Orion, then Canis Major, and then Sirius. Strangely, Sirius looked duller than usual.

An acrid smell hit me, carried on the stiff breeze. A thick haze hovered over the forest. In the clearing, I saw flickering movement. A knot of worry tightened in my stomach.

An orange glow pierced the haze—the glow of flames dancing. I heard shouts below. I thought of the two hunters. Likely they were up, stoking the fire, cooking their breakfast, that's all. But I knew this was unlikely. The flames were too widespread for such a simple explanation.

The shouts grew louder. Out of the haze, racing to the ridge, three figures emerged. Butch first, the chain clanking behind him. Then Ted and Sam, rifle and bow across their shoulders.

"What an idiot you are!" Sam screamed. He ran behind Ted, his belly swaying with each step.

"Aw, shut up. You were no help, were you?" Ted yelled back.

Fanned by the wind, the fire charged across the parched clearing. With flames licking behind, Butch galloped ahead. Ted chased the chain and yelled, "Wait up, Butch!"

The three tore past weeds and wove around boulders. They charged up the steep grade that led to the top of the ridge. I looked for a place to hide, but the ridge was bare of trees with little more than a slab and some brush to break the monotony. I flattened myself on the ground behind a bush, hoping I wouldn't be noticed.

Butch arrived at the top first. His tongue hung from his mouth like a soggy tie. Slobber drizzled to the ground. The two men followed, panting and clutching their sides.

"Now what?" Ted said.

The other man didn't answer. Sam backed away from the edge of the ridge and shook his head.

Just then, Butch saw me. He growled. It was a weak, muted growl as if Butch felt it was his duty to threaten me even though he didn't have the stomach for battle.

I studied Butch. Eyes wide. Tail hanging lifeless. Shoulders hunched. Butch was scared.

"What the...?" Ted saw me, too.

Sam looked. "Whaddya know. A weenie dog. What's he doing here?"

A loud explosion shifted their attention. At the edge of the clearing where grass met the forest, a pine tree burst into flames. Fire leaped up the trunk into the upper branches. Embers shot skyward. Some landed on other trees, spawning new fires. Others spiralled upward, carried by the wind farther into the forest. One ember landed at Ted's feet.

"Where do we go?" he said, stamping it to death.

Sam peered at the wall of rock behind them. "Not sure. We should be okay here, don't ya think?"

"I hope so," Ted pressed his back against the wall. "There's not much on the ridge that can burn, is there?"

Sam shrugged. "Just us and that stupid weenie dog."

Ted wiped his forehead with his sleeve. He grabbed Butch's chain and pulled the dog closer. "You'll be okay, Butch."

Then Ted did the strangest thing. He ran his hand along Butch's back, patted the dog, and hugged him. Then he unleashed Butch. The chain clattered to the ground. "You're free to go, Butch."

"What are you doing?" Sam said.

My question, too. I backed away and looked for an escape route.

Ted gazed at Sam. "What am I doing? Setting Butch loose. He'll have a much better chance on his own, don't you think?"

Flames gobbled brush in the clearing and ignited tinder-dry trees. Butch peered at the fire, then he studied Ted's face. He nudged Ted's leg and wagged his tail. Finally, he sat on his haunches at Ted's feet.

Ted pushed him away. "Go, you crazy mutt. Come on. Scoot while you have the chance."

But Butch wouldn't leave. He moved closer to Ted and gazed ahead.

Funny how the mind works. Fear left me. I pictured

Sirius, loyal to Prince Yudhistira. Butch wasn't much different. Would he earn a star in heaven, too?

A surge of heat and the smoke hit us. "Hey, mutt," Sam called above the roar of the flames. "Better join us."

"Yeah. You'll be a roasted weenie if you don't hurry."

"Roasted weenie! Good one, Ted."

Butch woofed. He seemed to be calling me over, too. But I thought of Mike. The route to Madison lay below. In a few moments, flames would cut off any chance of reaching Jess.

I ran down the slope.

"Hey, weenie," Sam called. "Are you nuts? Come back!"

Chapter 44

On the way down, I dodged thistles thick with burrs. I avoided sizzling embers. At the bottom, I entered the forest. Smoke hovered above the ground. An orange haze dulled the usual forest green. The sweltering heat made breathing difficult.

In that instant, I regretted my decision. I pictured another time and place. The birthday party. I knew fire, the speed at which it spreads, the damage it leaves in its wake, the pain it causes. I turned to go back up to the ridge, back to safety with Ted, Sam, and Butch.

But then I imagined Mike lying on the ground, breathing hard, his heart thudding unevenly. I thought of Zach and Emma, shivering and afraid. I thought of Jess, waiting and worrying. They were all counting on me. I couldn't let them down.

I visualized the terrain as I had viewed it from the ridge—the stream, rail line, far-off Madison. They all lay at the outer edge of the forest.

I took a deep breath, knowing it might have to last a while. Through the haze, I saw a gap between the trees. I aimed for it. I ran for my life. I ran for the others. I ran to the stream I knew was there,

The trees were so close, the branches seemed to be shaking hands with each other. Flames whooshed from one tree to another. The forest boomed with pops and crashes. A surge of heat hit my rear.

I glanced back. It was a brief look, just long enough to confirm my fears. The fire was gaining ground, moving faster than I could run. I barrelled on, knowing that this was the only option.

With every step, my joints ached. The burrs chafed my belly. Sharp rocks jutted from the ground. I dodged some but couldn't avoid others. Old wounds reopened. Fresh ones appeared. My torn pads bled again.

I wove between shadowy trees, through a haze growing thicker. When I couldn't see, I tapped into instinct. When hope dwindled, I kept the end goal in sight. Mike, Zach, Emma—they needed me.

Then, the inevitable happened. I tripped over a root. The smoke was so heavy that I didn't see it until it was too late. I stumbled and fell. A jolt of pain shot up my leg, then for a moment, I felt nothing.

I must have blacked out. Probably for just a second. Long enough anyways.

I've heard people say that when you are about to die, scenes from your life flicker by.

In that moment, it happened to me. It was like watching a slide show, only the images flashed by so quickly that I couldn't make out the pictures. They were blurred and out of focus. Then the slide show jerked to a sudden stop. A frame froze. The blurriness lifted. I saw Buck, Sparky, and the others at Derby. I saw Ruth. Then, I saw Mike.

The slide show played forward, slowly this time. It moved ahead and stopped. I saw myself sitting with Mike under the stars on the night he told me the story of Svana. Then the slide show continued. I saw myself beside Mike's bench outside, keeping him company as he gazed at the globe and its four figures.

That scene faded. Another took its place. I saw myself on the living room floor, watching Laika, the astronaut dog, on TV. Then, in the next scene, I was in the kitchen, midway across the floor, yipping at Lucinda on the counter.

On it went. The slide show zipped ahead. Sometimes it moved backwards. It stopped at different scenes. Mike reading the story of Balto and his heroic run across Alaska. Me leading Zach and Emma home in the dead of night. Mike reading the story of Bobbie, the Wonder Dog. Me beside the roaring stream, leaving Mike, Zach, and Emma to find Jess.

Just then, the slide show stopped. A movie started. I saw myself on the floor beside Mike's bed. Mike had *Everything Dogs* open. I heard Mike's voice, soft and gravelly. "You're special, aren't you, Coop?" Then he started reading the story of Salty. When he finished, he turned to me. "Pretty remarkable, don't you think?" I heard him say it as if he was right there.

Then, the flashback ended. It seemed to have lasted hours, but it must have only been a moment.

I heard a roar. I saw a flash. I felt pain on my flank. I wasn't dead. Not yet.

I rolled to extinguish the flames scorching my back.

Chapter 45

A tree behind me thudded to the ground, spewing sparks and ash. All around, trees blazed.

What was I supposed to make of the flashback, of these glimpses from my life? If there was a message, what was it? But almost as soon as the question surfaced, I knew the answer. Like Sirius and Bobbie, I had been loyal to my owner. Like Laika and Balto, I had persevered. Like Salty...

Mike's words came back to me. "You're special, aren't you, Coop?" Salty had led his blind owner down the stairs of the World Trade Center, through smoke and past fire to safety. He must have felt fear. He must have thought his life was coming to an end. He didn't just wait for it to happen. He did something for himself and for Omar.

I peered through the smoke and flames. There was no passageway through the fire, just flames leaping on all sides. Then I noticed a dark space beside a fallen log nearby. A burrow, probably made by a woodchuck or badger.

For once, my size worked in my favour. A large dog like Butch or Buck could never have done it. But I did. I wriggled to force myself into the tight opening. I clawed to scoop out dirt and widen it. Once inside, the cavity fanned out into a series of broad tunnels.

Some went sideways. Others headed downwards. I dug myself as deep into the tunnel as I could.

An enormous whoosh filled the burrow. A surge of heat followed. Smoke filled the cavity. I tunnelled deeper to find fresh air. I spread my body against the cool soil. I thought of Salty. I thought of Mike. Mostly, I waited, held my breath, and trembled.

Eventually, the roar of the flames lessened. The smoke thinned. I heard a chop-chop sound growing louder and then buzz of an airplane. I heard sizzles and pops. Suddenly, water swamped the tunnel, dousing the flames. In an instant, the dirt around me turned into a slurry of red mud and ash.

I couldn't breathe. I couldn't see either. As I clawed back out of the tunnel, I gulped mud. When I finally emerged, drenched and filthy, my coat was the colour of rust. I shook off as much of the dirt and fire retardant as I could. I inhaled the smoky air and gazed at charred trunks, soggy ash, and wisps of smoke that spiralled skyward.

The chop-chop sound grew louder. Through the haze, I spotted a helicopter swinging a bucket overhead. When the chop of the helicopter faded, I heard other sounds. Butch barking. Excited cries of relief from the two men on the ridge. And other sounds, too. The thunder of a stream. Then, the squeal of wheels.

The rail line.

I followed the sounds, running as fast as I could. Ahead, I saw the bridge still standing over the roaring stream. A train rolled lazily across it, gaining speed with every spin of its wheels.

A steep, slick bank led to the bridge. I charged up, only to lose my footing right away. Back I slid.

A memory flashed into my mind—the night I joined Mike for the first time on the bed. It too had been a daunting climb, but I'd made a run for it then, dug my paws into the folds, and plotted a route up the slick fabric to the top.

Why not try the same thing here?

Rather than tackle the steep grade head-on, I planned a route that wound between clumps of brush. I still slid, but the clumps provided some traction, enough to make it to the top.

When I reached the bridge, I followed the train as it chugged down the line. I ran after it as the helicopter swept past with another load of water. I kept my sights on it even when the train pulled far ahead and became a dot along the horizon.

Again I thought of Mike, Emma, and Zach. Were they safe? The wind had pushed the fire to the east, away from them. I glanced back. The helicopter and plane were still circling, dumping water and fire retardant to end the blaze.

By now, the train had disappeared. I plodded on. To Madison. To Jess.

To Jess? I stopped. Where was Jess? How would I find her? I'd never been to Madison before.

I shook off the worry. I'd come too far, endured too much to give up now. I'd find Jess somehow.

Madison appeared along the horizon, a cluster of

tiny buildings nestled below towering mountains. Jess was right. It was beautiful. Peaceful. A safe place far from Rick. It looked exactly like the photos that Jess had shown us.

I pictured that moment. Jess at the table. All of us huddled around. Map spread open. Photos of the house, barn, and yard around it. The house—a two storey with a sagging porch, white with faded green trim. The barn—set behind, leaning, and a little shabby. A short fence with pickets missing enclosed the yard. And horses. Yes, there were horses, too.

"It's a quiet place, just outside of town, not far from the rail line," I remembered Jess saying.

I trudged on, a little faster now. I passed a house set far into the surrounding forest. It had no barn, no fence. Not Jess's. I kept going, checking each of the properties I passed.

The town loomed ahead, getting closer with each step. Had I missed Jess? I began to doubt myself. Maybe I had gotten it wrong.

I drew up the mental picture again. House. Barn. Yard. Horses.

A soft whinny broke through my thoughts. I heard the thump of hooves striking the ground. I turned. Off to the side, hidden behind a cluster of trees, I caught a glimpse of white. A two storey house, white with green trim. A barn. And horses.

Two horses hung their heads over the fence. They stared right at me, ears twitching. I could almost hear their thoughts. *Well, finally you're here. Now what?*

Chapter 46

Lucky for me, Jess was home. She found me at her doorstep, barking like I'd never barked before.

"Coop? I've been so worried."

Dark circles rimmed her eyes. Her clothes were rumpled as if she'd slept in them. Her eyes narrowed as she studied me. "What a mess you are." Then she peered past me and bit her lip. "Where are the others?"

I barked again. What else could I do?

Jess ran to the end of the long driveway. I followed, limping slowly. Jess gazed down the road, then she did the same with the rail line. When she spotted the smoke that hovered like a black cloud in the distance, she drew a deep breath. Her shoulders slumped. She swung around. "What happened, Coop?"

Jess picked me up, ignoring the sludge that coated my fur. As she cradled me in her arms, her fingers grazed the burrs on my belly. They lingered on my scar before moving on to the singed patch of fur beyond. I winced and yipped. The wound was still fresh.

"Coop! You poor thing."

Jess sniffed my fur and wrinkled her nose. Her lip trembled. "Where are Zach and Emma? Where's Dad?"

She ran her fingers down my neck. "What's this?"

I'd almost forgotten about the earbuds and the note. Jess's fingers shook as she untied the stained page. "Zach's," she said as she read the message.

She looked down the rail line again. "Come, Coop. Show me."

The horses neighed as if they were part of the conversation. *Yeah, Coop. Show her.*

We jumped in the car and tore down the road, me in the passenger seat, Jess manning the wheel. Jess wiped away a small tear, then clenched her jaw. "Let's find them."

Jess drove like Mike, heavy on the gas pedal and light on the brakes. We tore down the gravel road, spewing spirals of dust. Stones pinged the underside as we bounced over ruts and whipped around curves.

Jess glanced at the earbuds and Zach's note. She turned sharply onto a narrow, paved road. A few miles later, she turned again. We rocketed down another road, narrower and rougher than the last. I hung on, paws gripping the door as familiar terrain zipped past. Trees. Rocks. A stream, mighty and powerful that seemed to follow the road.

Jess recited numbers as we bounced over cracks in the pavement. "Mile 10…Mile 11…" She looked at Zach's note again. "We're looking for mile marker 15."

I barked, eager to help. When Jess pulled over, I barked even louder.

"Mile 15." Jess pointed to a sign beside the road. "Is this it, Coop?"

Tire tracks etched in the dirt led down to the water. Where they met the rocks along the bank, they disappeared. I barked again. *Yes. This is it.*

Jess peered across the stream to the thick forest beyond. She pulled out her cellphone. "You sure, Coop?"

Jess paced along the bank. She yelled, "Zach! Emma! Dad!" But her voice was swept away, lost to the thundering rapids.

After a long wait, police arrived, sirens blaring and lights flashing. Firefighters followed. With ropes and harnesses, they forged the stream. I watched from shore as they threaded through the woods on the other side. Many minutes later, a blast from a whistle pierced the forest, followed by screams.

"They're here!"

I can't say that I fully understood what followed, but Jess did. I saw it in her eyes. I heard it in her voice. And I smelled it. I smelled her relief. I smelled her sadness.

After rescuers carried Emma across to safety, Jess hugged her tight and wiped away her tears. Zach was next. Jess hugged him, too. Zach hugged back, his hands trembling. Even Lucinda, who arrived after, wild-eyed and clinging to a firefighter, received a hug.

I circled Zach and Emma and pawed their legs to show I was glad, too.

Zach bent down to pet me. "Coop, you really came through. I knew you would." A tear drifted down his cheek. Zach wiped it away. "He would have been so proud of you."

Zach looked across the stream. Then he turned to look at Jess. I looked, too.

Jess was talking to the firefighter. The man took off his helmet. He bowed his head. Jess gasped. Her hand flew to her mouth. "No!" she shouted.

Chapter 47

Dogs aren't normally allowed at funerals. That's what the funeral director told Jess, but she insisted and he finally agreed. "Okay, the dog can come, but only to the cemetery, understand?"

Mike wouldn't have wanted anything fancy. I'm pretty sure Jess didn't want Rick to find out either, so it was a simple affair with only a few close friends. Sophie was one. When she saw me, she flashed a weak smile.

"You're going to miss him, aren't you?" she said, reaching to pat my head.

Funny about that. I wanted to bark at her, even nip her hand. Some resentments are not easily forgotten. But I held back. I let Sophie muss my fur. This was Mike's time, not mine. I owed him that much and more.

Mike was buried between Eva and Johnny. I thought it was a fitting place. Jess sniffled throughout the graveside service and dabbed her eyes with a tissue. Emma clung to her mother. Zach stood beside Jess, one arm around her, the other holding my leash.

For most of the service, I held it together. So did Zach. It was beautiful day for a funeral, sunny and warm, but not too hot. A soft breeze rustled the trees, adding a soothing touch to the scene. It was almost as if Mike was there, breathing in and out with the wind.

I thought of Mike, how he'd been preparing for this, how he'd missed Eva, how he'd been separated from Johnny for so long. Was he with them now? I thought so, but then what do I know? I am only a dog.

I hung back after the others left. It was only Zach and me then. Zach must have known what I wanted, what I needed. Perhaps he needed it, too. He unleashed me. "Go ahead, Coop. It's okay."

I'm not sure why, but at that moment, I thought of Butch and Ted. Butch wouldn't leave his owner even when he had the chance. He stuck by Ted, loyal to the end.

I lay in the dirt beside Mike one last time.

I whimpered. Then I howled.

Zach let me stay for a long time.

Chapter 48

After the funeral, everything changed. Jess sold Mike's house. We stayed there, cleaning and sifting through Mike's belongings before the new owners moved in. I half expected Rick to show up. But he didn't. As far as I could tell, he didn't know that Mike had died or that Jess and the kids were moving to Madison. I pictured him still in his car, following the truck with Zach's cellphone inside, weaving down endless highways that led nowhere.

Jess sorted Mike's things into piles, some to keep for herself, others to sell at an estate sale, still others to donate or send to the landfill. Zach and Emma helped—sort of. They were easily distracted, Zach with games on the new phone that Jess purchased for him, Emma with Lucinda, who seemed to be losing weight from her many attempts to escape.

Everything carried a memory of Mike. More than once, I caught Jess standing still, her eyes gazing at an item in her hand. "Did I ever tell you…" she'd say to the kids. Then she'd stop, a smile on her lips. She'd gently put the object down and pick up another. "I remember when…" she'd say, starting over.

What Jess kept and what she didn't keep mystified me. She kept the cracked teapot that Mike used every day but donated the electric kettle. She kept the framed pictures beside his bed but sold the table that held them. She pored through the books in Mike's room, sighed, and packed them into boxes to take to Madison, but she left the heavy bookcase that took up an entire wall.

Jess also kept many of Mike's tools. "They might come in handy some day," she told Zach.

Zach nodded, but I am not sure he really heard his mother. He was quiet, often distant, but I understood. It takes time to get over shock, to mend wounds that run deep, and even though Zach and Emma were both seeing counsellors, Zach especially seemed to carry a heavy burden. I think he blamed himself, that he didn't do enough to help Mike, that maybe he was responsible in some way for Mike's death.

I knew better. If anyone was to blame, it was me. I failed Mike. I didn't bring the help he needed in time to save him. Mike had rescued me, but I couldn't rescue him, and that was my burden to carry.

But even that didn't ring true. If Mike were here, he'd set the record straight. I know he would. "Nobody's to blame," he would say in that familiar gravelly voice. "It was simply my time."

One afternoon, soon after the funeral, Zach spread my blanket on the kitchen floor.

"Here, I saved it for you," he said, straightening out the edges.

I circled it, sniffed the familiar odours, scanned the familiar stains, lingered over the burn hole. The blanket seemed less inviting than before. As if I didn't need it like I once did. As if I'd outgrown it.

"Go on, Coop," Zach said.

I sat beside the blanket and gazed at the sink where Mike once stood, at the door where he once entered, at the table where he sat each morning to check his blood pressure. I remembered all of those times. I didn't need the blanket to hold those memories.

Zach understood. He folded the blanket and put it in a box along with a dozen other items destined for the landfill.

"That's that then," he said.

On the morning before the new owners took possession, a moving truck rumbled into the driveway. While two men loaded boxes and furniture, Zach and Emma took me for a walk. We wove down streets, past the Asian restaurant with its delicious smells, past the firehouse with its flapping flag, past the empty schoolyard. Soon we were at the busy highway.

"Do you know the way back?" Emma asked.

"Course I do," Zach answered.

"You said that before."

"I remember."

So did I. This time, it was different. So much had happened. I had changed. So had the others, especially Zach. He rarely yelled or cursed now. He seemed more confident, more mature. Like he'd already started turning his lemons into lemonade.

By the time we returned, the moving truck was

gone. Jess packed a few potted plants into the car and stepped back to gaze at the house for the last time.

"So this is it," she said, turning around. "Come, Coop."

She opened the car door. She ushered me inside while Zach and Emma claimed the back seat, one on each side of Lucinda's kennel.

As we wheeled out of the driveway, a strange thought occurred to me. Where were we going? *Please, not Derby*, I prayed.

Well past midnight the next day, we pulled into Jess's driveway. The moving truck had already come and gone. While Jess and the kids unpacked the car, I circled the yard, peeing in well-chosen spots.

After the long ride, I relished the fresh air. I investigated every patch, every corner. I savoured the smells hidden in the dirt. Each one told me about previous visitors—the deer that stopped to nibble the shrubs, the mice that scurried away, the horses that thundered by.

I could have stayed out there forever. There was a calmness about the place, a stillness. I looked up. There were more stars here than in the city. They seemed larger and brighter, too—like floodlights instead of the usual tiny light bulbs.

From the corner of my eye, I saw a flash, a trace of movement. A lighted object floated across the sky, etching an arc through the dark.

I held my breath. Laika. Was that her? Still orbiting the earth? In my heart I knew it wasn't. It was probably a meteorite making an appearance, but I followed its movement anyway. When it neared a cluster of stars, it seemed to stop before moving on. I looked closer. I'd never noticed that cluster before. Three stars. Two large ones with a smaller one nestled between them.

"Coop, come here," I heard Zach call. "I want to show you something."

I followed him around the house. In the starlit shadows, a bench waited. Mike's bench. Zach sat down and motioned for me to come closer. He dropped his hand to scratch my ears. "See." He pointed ahead.

Out of the darkness, a form emerged. A large globe made of twisted metal standing on a stone pedestal. Mike's globe.

"You can visit any time," Zach said.

I leaned forward to see better. Inside the globe stood four familiar figures—a woman, a tall man with his arm wrapped around her, and, standing in front, two young children—a boy and a girl.

I looked again. Something was different. There was a fifth figure inside. Mike's last creation. The dog that looked like me—long body, floppy ears, thin tail with a patch along its hindquarters and a star floating above its head.

The five figures looked hopeful and happy, as if the whole world was theirs, as if anything was possible.

Mike's words came back to me. *We can't change the past. We can only move forward.*

"Welcome home," Zach said.

THE END

Author's Note

Why write a book about a dog, told by a dog? I've been asked that several times. In fact, I've asked myself the same question. Yes, why? And why a dachshund of all breeds?

In part, the answer lies along Gateway Trail, a rugged, stone-pocked hiking trail in the McDowell Preserve region of Scottsdale, Arizona. Gateway is one of my favourite hikes, not only because it is rugged and scenic, but also because on any given day you are bound to encounter dogs who are out for a jaunt with their human companions. Weekends are especially popular with dog-human teams, and for dog-watchers like me, it's not only entertaining, but also inspiring. Canines of all shapes, sizes and breeds make the trek. If they can do it, why not me?

One Saturday, I spotted a dachshund at the trail-head. He was decked out in a green sweater and tethered to a young man. I'd never seen a dachshund on Gateway before, and this dog looked particularly eager to start the hike. I thought of the challenges he faced ahead—the steep climb, the many steps he would have to take with his short legs, and the sharp stones that might slice into his pads. I thought of the resilience the dog would need, the strength and determination it would take to make the climb with a body like his.

Later, at the midway point, as Jo and I enjoyed a break, I spotted the young man as he chugged up the trail shouldering his backpack. I looked for the dachshund but couldn't see him. Had he given up? Did the young man leave him behind? When the man passed us, my questions were answered. Peering out of the backpack, ears flapping with each of the young man's steps, was the dachshund. If dogs can wear smiles, I'm sure this one did. See, he seemed to be saying, there's more than one way to skin a cat.

The story of a small dog with a cynical edge who pits himself against challenges was born that day. When it came to the selection of my lead character, I knew it had to be a dachshund. And who better to tell the story than the dog himself?

I have many to thank for helping me to write this book. First and foremost, the family and friends who stood guard, feeding me encouragement throughout the long process. You bolstered me when I staggered and supported me when I doubted my choice of subject.

I am also indebted to the members of my writing group, The Anita Factor, who offered suggestions, asked important questions, and coached me when I faltered. Thank you Christina Janz, Deborah Froese, Gabriele Goldstone, Jodi Carmichael, MaryLou Driedger, Melanie Matheson, Melinda Friesen, Pat Trottier and Suzanne Goulden.

Although Derby Animal Shelter is a fictional entity, it is based largely on my visits to Foothills Animal Rescue in Scottsdale, Arizona. I owe a debt of gratitude to the kind folks there who answered my questions and toured me through the facility.

The team of experts at Great Plains Publications who saw promise in the story and spirited me to the finish line, deserve my gratitude, too. Thanks Catharina de Bakker, Stephanie Berrington, and Mel Marginet.

Dogs have played important roles in my life. As I wrote the story, it seemed to me that they were somehow at my side, feeding me lines and guiding my hand. Coop is a composite of all of them, so to Benji, Bernie, Freckles, Roxy, Lilah, Hayley and Molly, thank you not only for providing me with an abundance of material, but also for the joy you've brought into my life.

Finally, to Jo, my wife, who was beside me on the hike that inspired the story and who counselled me when I stumbled writing it, I can honestly say "I couldn't have done it without you!" Thanks, Jo.